THREE WISE MEN
(A Christmas Anthology)

By:

Nancy Ricker

Jan Romes

Laura Ricker

Cover Design: Tugboat Design
Formatting: Tugboat Design
www.tugboatdesign.net

My gift to those who challenged me and believed in me!
~ Nancy Ricker

To everyone looking for love this Christmas!
~ Jan Romes

To those who believe in true love and all that it stands for!
~ Laura Ricker

Alex, Nick, and Evan

<u>Three men who need to wise up for love!</u>

Three unique stories told by three unique writing voices!

Enjoy!

Midnight Magic

ALEX

By: Nancy Ricker

Chapter One

I lost my best friend eight years ago today. It was a life changing moment that seemed unbearable at the time. You never know what path this world will take you down, but I feel like I am stumbling. I am no longer steady on my feet, and now I am only half of what once was whole. My life, my future is uncertain. I miss him so much. The center of my heart remains empty as I continue to grieve for him. It does not get any easier as some may predict. Accepting the fact that your hopes and dreams planned together are now unreachable alone is a difficult bridge to cross.

Many of the depressing details escape me, and I blame my fogginess on the tremendous amount of stress I was under. My dearest friend, Rose, once told me, "Olivia, if God brings you to it, He will bring you through it." Rose is my rock and my sturdy sounding board. Someone I can always depend on. If I need to call in the middle of the night because I can't sleep, she'll come running. We may sip hot tea or warm milk until slumber comes. I would often find her the next morning asleep on the couch. She stayed without asking, knowing I would sleep better if I was not alone. When I don't feel like talking because I'm feeling a little sorry for myself, she understands and does not criticize.

We have an eerie closeness that is hard to explain. If I'm thinking about Rose and make myself a promise to call her later, the phone rings with her reassuring voice on the other end of the line. Two Christmas's ago, I bought her a lovely ceramic angel figurine. We laughed together when I opened her gift which was an angel as well – a silver necklace with a shiny angel pendant. Our thoughts are often the same and we frequently finish each other's sentences. This friendship is truly one of a kind. She has seen me at my worst and still loves me anyway. Rose understands my heartache.

I never dreamed I would have to go through anything like this without him. This was something I never prepared for. It has changed me. Alex was my world, my loving companion, my reason for looking forward to each new day. He was a great man, friend and lover. He was the husband every mother dreamed to life for her daughter. I want to do everything possible to keep his memory alive, but you can't wrap your arms around a memory.

He was the strong, silent type. Physically strong as a result of hard work on the family farm and a dedication to a daily exercise regimen. Mentally strong from always reading with a quick wit and an intriguing memory which I seem to lack. Silent when it came to sharing his worries, his fears and his feelings. Yet there was a soothing softness in his silence. A quiet understanding between us when kind and caring thoughts were touchingly conveyed by a loving look or a warm embrace. I have come to know that silence can be golden. Even so, this was the trait that at times made loving him a challenge. Trying to read his mind without misunderstanding what was hiding in the corners there. Understanding meaningful words that often went unspoken. Knowing when my own peaceful silence was also necessary and welcomed.

But make no mistake, I never doubted his love. Love to him meant taking out the garbage without being reminded two or three times a day, or bringing me fresh cut flowers from my blooming garden. Love could be the act of changing the oil in my car and checking the tires or taking me to the Dairy Queen for a hot fudge sundae. Love might say, "Olivia, you're a great cook," instead of "I love you." Even though it was difficult for Alex to express, I certainly could feel it. It felt like contentment. It felt like trust. It was a comfortable, warm feeling always near my heart. It made me feel safe. It was what I dreamed love should feel like. I miss it. I want to fall in love again!

Chapter Two

They should have named me Oliver, instead of Olivia. I was definitely the tomboy of our small town neighborhood. You would be more likely to find me playing pitch and catch with the boys than playing dolls and dress-up with the girls. My two older brothers didn't mind me tagging along. They relished an opportunity to tease their buddies that the girl that just beat them was their baby sister!

I wasn't afraid to get dirty either. Peter, Thomas, and I would walk four blocks to where the water-filled ditch entered town. There, we would slip and slide up and down the bank in search of insects, amphibians and reptiles to collect and raise as pets. Our parents often scolded us for playing at our favorite spot. They were tired of finding critters hiding in our bedroom and tired of treating the three of us for bites, bruises and itchy poison ivy.

I disliked my weekly chores of tedious house cleaning and laundry, and Mom sure had a hard time getting me into a frilly dress. Sunday church was the only time I had no choice in the matter. Dad taught the boys how to mow and trim the grass, to rake and how to use the common tools. They were lucky to have outdoor chores that got cancelled whenever it rained.

Our home was located on Fourth Street. It was within walking distance to school, church, and the corner grocery that had a satisfying selection of penny candy that we would spend our weekly allowance on. Jawbreakers and bubble gum were my favorites. We had a large back yard that served as the neighborhood playground. Our parents didn't mind, they said at least they knew where we were…most of the time.

The two-bedroom Cape Cod was small but charming. The white windows and trim on the gray clapboard siding gave it a neat, clean appearance. The back porch was large enough for a white, wooden swing and two Adirondack chairs. Window boxes overflowed with colorful blooms that lasted all summer long, and the giant oak tree on the west side of the house created the perfect shady oasis for summertime picnics or autumn frolics in the scratchy leaves.

The kitchen was cozy and always had wonderful aromas of fresh baked cookies, brownies or pies emanating from it. The living room was small which explains why Mom and Dad always chased us outside to play. Our bedroom was shared, giving the boys the most desired bunk bed and I slept under the pink flowered quilt that covered my twin bed near the window.

Mom and Dad had their hands full raising three rambunctious children, but they had a plan and made a great team. As children we thought they were strict, but their goal was to instill in us the groundwork for success. They taught us the value of responsibility and accountability, honesty and trust. Education, manners and physical activity were not overlooked, but family, friends and faith were the base of strength that all else was built on. They led by example and we admired them, respected them and we loved them.

* * *

Alex was lucky to be raised on a spacious farm three miles from town. His dad and three brothers worked hard and worked well together to run the five-hundred acres of rich, dark soil that had been in the Rousch family for three generations. Unfortunately, his mother was no longer in the family picture. Elizabeth was only thirty-four when she was diagnosed with inoperable lung cancer even though she never smoked a day in her life. This cruel and terrifying disease was kind in that it took her more quickly than most. Her suffering was kept at a minimum and for that they were grateful. Alex's dad, Charles, was her loyal caregiver and quickly learned the art of nursing and he was thankful that he was able to keep her home among her favorite things until she peacefully drifted into her next life.

Because there was no female presence in the house, the boys were challenged at a young age to learn the domestic arts of cooking, cleaning, laundry and shopping. Dad was proud of them when they didn't argue about it. They understood that it would only hurt him more. He said, "This experience will make you better husbands one day." They believed him.

Charles talks about his wife and mother of his children on a regular basis and tells loving stories about the numerous photographs scattered throughout the house. He will never let the boys forget her and what she meant to the family. It is still obvious how much he loved her.

Farming was all Alex knew back then. He didn't know the other boys his age were hanging out at the baseball field near school or at the ice cream shop teasing the pretty girls. Some would tempt him and say that he didn't know what he was missing. Although he was curious, Alex reported home directly after school and was satisfied with his childhood there.

Even though there was always work to be done, life on the farm wasn't all work. They made time to fish in the secluded pond near the back woods. Bass and blue gill were the usual catch of the day and they were taught how to filet and fry them. Timed-challenges on the homemade obstacle course kept the competitive spirit alive in a friendly way and kept the boys in great physical shape.

The most fun came from riding vehicles of all shapes and sizes, not only the red Farmall tractor that Charles owned, but sleds and bicycles too. But the best ride ever was the surprise their dad gave them for Christmas one year. It was a used, rusty moped that they transformed into a mighty, mean, speedy dirt bike machine. They went through gallons of gas every week while the worn, treaded tires paved a lengthy dirt track where the grass used to be. The cloud of dust would be flying every evening until it became too dark for safety and they reluctantly reported to the house for showers and dreaded homework.

Their father understood that childhood play was an important part of growing up. It taught you valuable life lessons you didn't learn in a classroom. The Rousch young men learned how to share, how to save and that hard work paid off. They also learned how to settle differences without getting into a fist fight, although a few unavoidable brawls did break out from time to time.

The rewards of working the land is what settled in his bones. Alex understood the big picture. To watch the life cycle of crops from planting the small seed in the fresh tilled soil at just the right depth, to the sprouting and emergence above the earth's crust, to germination and finally production of wheat heads, bean pods and ears of corn. It was quite satisfying to know that you had a very small part in helping to feed the world.

He also learned the important role that Mother Nature played in the farmer's life. The weather was the usual topic of conversation when they went with their dad to the local elevator for supplies. There were always droughts or an overabundance of rain to complain about or maybe this year it might be an untimely frost, ice storm, wind or hail. Your entire season could be ruined by an infestation of a crop destroying pest or uncontrollable disease. Maybe this would be the year when the growing season was perfect and you'd be rewarded with record-setting yields, and life on the farm is suddenly worthwhile and profitable.

Chapter Three

You could say we were high school sweethearts. The time we spent together was simple, satisfying and sensual from the start. Our love story was not conceived by the love at first sight phenomenon. I do believe it exists, but it is not a common occurrence. Alex and I believe that love is friendship that has caught fire, and we are just beginning to rub the two sticks together. Many couples of our generation tell similar stories of a simple life with simple love.

The quiet life lived in the gentle, rolling hills of Pennsylvania left little opportunity for adventure in the charming, small town of Hanover. There were larger cities nearby, either York or Gettysburg, but those of us with lack of transportation were destined to settle for what the immediate locale had to offer. The center of our universe in the 1940's happened to be the public high school located on Carlisle Street. All of our friends and neighbors attended there and before you were seventeen, most couples had already begun to evolve. Olivia Benford and Alexander Rousch were no exception.

We discovered early in our relationship that we had many things in common. We had fun when we were together, laughing at the same things. Alex was good at telling jokes and he and his buddies were usually guilty of planning harmless pranks. They spent their Friday nights soaping car windows, TP'ing the houses with the most trees and bushes, getting bonus points if it rained before morning, or planting an occasional potato in the tailpipe of their current enemy.

The two of us would rather spend our free time outdoors riding bicycles, walking or just sitting on a park bench watching the people go by. On a rainy day you could find either of us curled up with a good book. Reading is a favorite pastime of mine. To me, reading is not only educational but also entertaining. It can take you places you have never been, or make you nervous wondering how the plot will end, or surprise you when your favorite character turns out to be the villain, or warm your heart when the touching romance has a happy ending.

Frequent warm summer nights were spent together on my family's back porch talking without end, but also listening to the birds, locusts or crickets sweetly singing. Tranquil sunsets watched from there were breathtaking. No forests or city landscapes to block the view of the bright yellow sun changing to a glowing orange and crimson red. Swirls of pink and orange fading to blue and purple. A blessing to behold as the distorted orb meets the horizon – each day's reward if you take the time to notice.

One thing you could always count on was seeing each other every Sunday attending church with our families. Alex and I felt a special connection as a result. We were very much aware of the path this romance was on and wanted to be patient and enjoy the journey. We wanted to make sure we were headed in the right direction and avoid getting lost in each other. We needed to know the difference between love and lust. There is absolute truth in the notion that no one has the power to make you happier than the right man or more miserable than the wrong one.

Initially, there was a shared physical attraction that was impossible to ignore. Alex was exceptionally fit, very athletic, every young girl's dream. His deep-set eyes were his most attractive feature, if I had to choose just one. Those baby blues could capture you and draw you in with only a brief glance and would challenge you to look away if you dared. But who would want to? If eye contact alone could kick your developing hormones into gear like that, you would eagerly wonder what a tender touch would do. It didn't take long for two teenagers experimenting with this current romantic encounter to find out.

This man I want to get to know is wise beyond his years when it comes to the opposite sex. I get the unmistakable feeling that this sexual curiosity of mine could be taken to a new level with anyone who had more experience than I had and that was very little. Was now the right time to take this step? Was Alex the right man?

His initial touch caused my skin to come alive in a way I had never felt before. It was electric! Every hair follicle seemed to wake up and take notice, but the indescribable tingling sensation was far more than skin deep. I longed for his touch and gave Alex the green light to continue the erotic exploration, and he was more than happy to oblige.

The physical adventures of this relationship were exciting, but our connection was deeper than that. We trusted each other completely and expected honesty and openness. Lying in any form or fashion was totally unacceptable, and promises made were not to be broken. Spirituality was never in doubt as we both maintained our faith in the Catholic Church we were baptized in. At times we were just playful and spontaneous. We enjoyed teasing each other at any given opportunity and knew how lucky we both were to have been blessed with the best sense of humor. We discovered that we actually were laughing more at ourselves requiring much less time begging for forgiveness.

Alex was a gentleman and politely asked, "May I call you Livy?" I giggled and agreed, "Sure, I love it." It was touching and felt natural to me. No one else ever called me that which made it something special and unique coming only from Alex. It was his term of endearment that pleased me when I heard it.

I was somewhat surprised by the interest Alex showed in me back then, but it made me the happiest girl in town. I would rate my physique as average. Certainly not the popular cheerleader type most young boys are attracted to. My petite frame was lean and I had a killer smile any dentist would be proud of. My auburn hair was cut in a fashionable bob and my hazel-green eyes were topped with a long set of dark lashes. The prominent protrusion in the center of my face was not quite a ski slope, but ranked high on my list of the top ten things I would change about myself. Unfortunately, it's a Benford family trait that I can thank Grandpa Miles for. If the size of my nasal septum wasn't problem enough, the emergence of multiple brown freckles over the summer months added more visual imperfections that I could certainly do without.

Even though subconsciously I would rather disown my nose, it was never a problem for Alex. He would sometimes tease me about it in a humorous way, but he could keenly sense when I tolerated enough. He would say to me, "Livy, I love your nose! It's not a big deal!" What I heard at that moment was 'big' and 'nose'. It's my obsession I guess.

But wait…go back…what was that four letter word? L-O-V-E. Yes, it sounded like love. Yes, it feels like love! This cute, young boy I think I love has turned into a handsome, mature man that I'm pretty sure I love even more. He knows me better than I know myself. He knows what it means to me every time we say hello and every time we say goodbye, and every time we say goodnight he always, without fail, tenderly lifts my face to his and softly kisses this protrusion in the center of my face and says, "I love you, Livy."

Chapter Four

Not too many engaged couples plan their wedding for the chilly month of December, yet it was the favorite time of the year for the future Mr. and Mrs. Alexander Rousch, so that decision was made without debate. Weddings then were fairly simple as far as pomp and circumstance goes. Times were pretty tough for awhile following the years after World War II. The country's success in the war made us all proud to be American. Area young men who had served returned to hometown welcomes and all night celebrations. These young men were brave enough to accept the risk of war and lucky enough to survive it. The nation stood strong in the eyes of the world and there was a new energy and higher ambitions. The future held the promise of great achievement and prosperity. The veterans and their wives settled down to make babies, and so will we.

Our wedding ceremony was a simple, intimate affair for only our closest friends and family. Cherished photographs to preserve the occasion were taken by my Aunt Jo, who made the four hour drive from Pittsburgh for our celebration. The sun was shining brightly throughout the day and the reflection off the fresh blanket of snow which had fallen the night before made the blissful scene sparkle like diamonds.

My dearest friend, Rose and her husband, Jonathan stood as our witnesses. They are our closest friends from high school and we still spend a lot of time together. In their younger days, Jonathan would join Alex at the farm to help complete his daily chores giving them a little more time to find trouble. They got their jollies by swinging from ropes in the barn and by using possums, birds and mice for target practice with their BB guns. Rose and I shared everything from clothes and books to hopes and dreams. Frequent sleepovers and pajama parties gave us hours and hours to compare notes about the boys and our versions of puppy love.

I thought we had agreed not to spend money on wedding gifts for each other due to the unpredictable times ahead. Alex confirmed, "I did not spend any money, Livy, but a wedding gift you shall have." He slowly reached into his pocket and revealed a black velvet jewelry box, removed the pendant it contained, and gently fastened it behind my neck as he placed a romantic, lingering kiss on my right shoulder. I was astonished by its brilliance and design. "Alex, it's beautiful. Where did you get this?" His bedroom eyes moistened as he explained, "It was my grandmother's. Gramps gave it to her on their wedding day. It meant everything to her." My heart began to swell. It meant the world to me as well. I reciprocated his kiss with one of my own which landed directly on his inviting, velvety lips. This rare, one-carat blue diamond represented the Rousch family tradition of deep and everlasting love. As we recited our vows and declared our commitment to each other, there was no doubt that we would share this joy 'til death do us part'.

There was no honeymoon planned, and we were content to begin our new life on the family farm. Since Alex was the oldest of the four boys, we were the obvious choice as the next generation to inherit the Rousch homestead. The two-story house had been well-maintained since it was first built in 1912. There were three bedrooms located on the second floor accessed by a staircase decorated with an intricate hand-carved wood railing. The first floor was divided into a roomy foyer, living room, formal dining room, a large kitchen and a suitable bathroom. There was a dark cellar below the house that served as a laundry room and pantry. The wrap-around porch gave the home a traditional farmhouse appearance and served as a gathering place for socializing and an observation deck for supervision of the farm activity. Over the winter months the fireplace with the oak beam mantel captured our attention and warmed us nightly.

We scrimped and saved what little we could and were able to make ends meet and turn our house into a home. Alex was very knowledgeable about running the family farm thanks to the teachings from the generations before him. He was a good mechanic and produced beautiful crops of corn, soybeans and wheat. I enjoyed my role as Betty Crocker and could put on a pretty good spread for my hardworking farmer who must have had a bottomless pit for a stomach. I used my spare time to nurture my vegetable garden which produced well enough to permit canning and freezing a fair amount of our food supply for the next year.

I also took pride in my numerous flowerbeds strategically placed around our home to provide a colorful showing that could be viewed through the windows from inside the home. Thanks to my green thumb, the results were spectacular and earned me many blue ribbons at the county fair. I found a niche for producing some of the prettiest and most fragrant hybrid tea roses. Two of my favorites were the Mister Lincoln Rose and the Sheer Bliss Rose. It's true these bloomers demand a little more attention, but they repay the affection with their elegant, eye pleasing display.

The years passed quickly and we learned each other's strengths and weaknesses and how to compromise. We were successful at making this marriage work because we put in a conscious effort that some couples take for granted. Unfortunately, we remained childless, not by choice. It was very disappointing to Alex and I, but we could not let it destroy us. We had to accept the reality that this dream of ours was not going to come true. That it was not in God's plan. Unexpected bumps in the road like this can have the effect of either tearing you apart or making you stronger. Luckily for us it was the latter. Over time we changed our dreams of having a family and in place of that renewed our commitment to each other. The release of this burden gave us a new energy and zest to spend the rest of our lives as husband and wife not father and mother.

Chapter Five

The dream of retirement doesn't exist for the family farmer. Farming is a commitment to a vocation that usually lasts a lifetime. Most farmers I know wouldn't want it any other way. Some farm families are lucky to be able to slow down as they age when the younger generation is able to assist and eventually take over the established business. The planting season and harvest are the most demanding and often result in work days that last from sunup to sundown. The modernization of farm equipment has helped tremendously to balance the workload and decrease the physical toll of those who work the soil. Alex has been blessed with good health overall, but is now having some back discomfort as a result of his life's work. I never hear him complain even though I see the pain in his face and in his posture.

When the winter season draws near and the fall harvest is complete, we find more time for each other, which explains why the winter months are our favorite. We enjoy the shorter days when the hours seem to last a little longer. More time spent inside allows some of our favorite pastimes to reappear. For Alex, more time for reading, and for me, more time to experiment in the kitchen with new recipes and to bake enough bread and sweets to share. Nothing makes the house smell better and a husband happier than fresh bread baking in the oven.

The winter weather can be unpredictable in the state of Pennsylvania. We've survived blizzards, ice storms and power outages. If your glass is half-full there is nothing more romantic than being snowbound with flickering candles for light and a crackling, cozy fire for warmth.

If we lived in a warmer, southern climate, I would miss the change of seasons. Spring always brings the promise of new life as the colors return with the emergence of budding trees and blooming flowers. The warmth of the summer sun allows for more outdoor living and is certainly good for the crops. The cooler, crispness of fall with the red, orange and gold patchwork of the hills is remarkable. But we welcome the winter wonderland. A fresh fallen snow is so clean and pure. The reflection of the suns' rays reveals more sparkle than fairy dust. The windbreak of evergreens seems to bow under the weight of a heavy snow. A brisk wind may sculpt new and unusual formations that can change from minute to minute. A thin layer of ice though treacherous underfoot gives the appearance of shimmering glass and forms different shapes and sizes of frozen icicles precariously hanging from every surface. The emergence of ice skates, sleds, snowballs and snowmen provide free and humorous entertainment. There seems to be more time for coffee and hot chocolate.

Matched with our favorite season is our favorite holiday, Christmas. The shopping, the wrapping, the mailing of cards are more than just a time-consuming chore. It's time you take to think fondly of each recipient. It's a time you may think more of what they would like rather than what they need. The spirit of giving is uplifting. Finding the perfect gift for that special person on your list makes you more excited than a child on Christmas morning. The traditions of baking cookies, caroling and midnight mass are always completed and shared with others who possess the Christmas spirit. It truly is the most wonderful time of the year.

Chapter Six

There is something about attending midnight mass that always felt magical. The peace and serenity you feel deep in your soul is very comforting and fulfilling. The church bells chime Christmas carols and hymns into the chilly air of the silent night. All is a little more perfect if you are lucky enough to have snow. The Christmas choir puts in many hours of extra practice during the holiday season which assures a quite moving musical tribute to celebrate Christ's birth. The thirty minute prelude of musical selections before midnight brings everyone to church early for that always special Christmas Eve tradition.

The effort put forth by the decorating committee took our breath away with arrangements of red and white poinsettias, evergreen trees and twinkling lights. Even more impressive was the nativity scene displayed near the sacristy. The figurines were nearly life-size and though they had shown some wear and tear over the years still did not fail to make an everlasting impression of the real meaning of Christmas. If you took the time to stand there and imagine, you were drawn into the story as it has been told for thousands of years.

In the dating world, showing up to midnight mass with a member of the opposite sex served immediate notice to the rest of the community that something serious was going on between the two of you. Alex and I loved going to church together at Christmastime. Both of us being raised by good German Roman Catholics who had settled in the Midwest rooted us deep in faith and spirituality. The instilled traditions of Sunday Mass, the Blessed Sacraments and The Ten Commandments were the center of our faith. These core values were something Alex and I unequivocally agreed on.

As a couple, we never missed midnight mass and chose this special time of year to reflect on what we had done for our marriage since the last time we had knelt there. We waited until all the other parishioners filed out of church to head home for some egg nog and visions of sugar plums. We would linger there alone in the silence near the sacristy and take in the meaningful scene before us. Hand in hand we spoke quietly about where our relationship was and where we would like it to go. Even though Alex was a man of few words, the discussion was lighthearted, pleasant and quite romantic as the lights dimmed overhead. When we realized that nearly an hour had passed, we would rise and express our thanks for the year's blessings and ask God to continue to watch over us as always. A serene embrace would follow and Alex would raise my chin to his and those soft lips would aim for mine, but traditionally ended up on the tip of my nose. "I love you, Livy," he whispered.

Chapter Seven

Alex and I are still in love—with each other, and with man's best friend, Max. He limped into our lives when he was just a pup who had unfortunately gotten a little too close to a rusty, old muskrat trap. Alex found him when he was mowing the drainage ditch that borders the back forty. He was bruised, wet and bleeding. He quickly freed Max and examined the wounds that needed some expert first aid. I watched with wonder from the kitchen window as I saw Alex approaching with a soft brown bundle cradled in his arms. I ran out to meet him. "I just found him, Olivia. Can you help?" He pleaded. One brief look and I hurried to the house for soap and water, iodine and gauze. We worked together to care for this stranger. The poor thing whimpered softly as we dressed his wounds. Max didn't appear to need stitches, but we planned a precautionary trip to the veterinarian for in the morning.

We fed Max some leftovers from dinner and he lapped up a bowl of water. He proceeded to curl up on the plush rug next to the garage door and made himself at home. Before long he was sound asleep. Alex and I looked at each other and could sense what was happening. A bond had already formed, and we had just adopted a new member into our family.

The trip to the vet was uneventful. Dr. Cooley said we did a good job mending his wounds and Max should heal nicely. He gave him a tetanus shot and sent us home with antibiotics. Doc also gave us strict instructions to return in four weeks for routine immunizations. The office would notify us if they received any reports of a missing puppy.

During the short drive home, we discussed nothing else but possible names for our new baby. Something strong and manly. "How about Max?" Alex said. It was perfect, with a meaningful connection to family. He would be named after gramps, Maxwell G. Rousch.

Sunday visits to Grandma and Gramps' were a favorite childhood memory for Alex that he often talked about. Listening to the long, entertaining stories that only Gramps could tell and dipping Grandma's prize-winning cookies in milk were fondly remembered. Gramps loved dogs and raised several loyal breeds over the years including a retriever of his own named Sienna.

Max was a smart dog, obedient and easily trained as golden retrievers are. He was good natured and affectionate. His rich, lustrous coat was a deep golden brown with reddish hues highlighted by the sun. His dark brown eyes could melt your heart even when he'd been a little mischievous. Max thought he was human. He quickly learned the tricks Alex taught him: to roll over, to shake and play dead. He would wait near the road for the paper boy and deliver the daily news to us even though a few slobbers covered the front page.

It was entertaining to watch Alex and Max play. Games of fetch with a thick twig that had fallen from an oak tree. Swims in the pond at the back of our property confirmed his love for the water. This game ended with a violent shake that purposely sent showers of water in Alex's direction. Humorous games of hide and seek that favored Max with his keen sense of smell and tracking talents. But Max's favorite game was Frisbee. He never tired of it and showed off his running and jumping abilities. At last count, I think we were on Frisbee number five.

Max lived the good life which ended after thirteen and a half years. He died of old age along with a little help from acute renal failure. We were just beginning to question whether it was time to humanely have him put down. We thank God for making that decision for us.

It broke our hearts to lose him, and yes, it felt like we lost a member of the family. I cried as I watched Alex construct a suitable wooden crate for burial and tearfully dig an appropriate grave. It was the hardest thing he ever had to do. Max was laid to rest along the back lot where now stands a colorful memory garden. He loved us unconditionally and expected nothing in return. He was truly loved…and lost. His memory is our keepsake.

Chapter Eight

My current home is not the one we shared for fifty-two years, but it's affordable on my meager social security budget and I'm comfortable here. It may be small, but it provides me with all the necessities. I manage to eat a fairly well-balanced diet which Dr. Powell routinely nags me about as he tries to keep me on track with my health. Trying to stay mobile and active is possible and convenient if I use the community gym just around the corner, and there always seems to be friendly, neighborly faces to socialize with; perhaps a stimulating game of cards, a relaxed dinner date, or simply passing the hours with quiet conversation and enjoyable reminiscing.

The room I spend most of my time in welcomes the morning sun through a large bay window. An interesting view with oak, elm and maple trees and a variety of flowering shrubs allow me to keep track of the four seasons as they pass ever too quickly now. The highlight in the landscaping is the flowerbed right outside my window that is home to the long stemmed rose bushes I planted two years ago, or was it four years ago? A fresh coating of new, pristine snow reminds me that my favorite time of year is quickly approaching.

I am surrounded by all of my favorite things. A small table for two is perfect for enjoying my daily cup-o-joe. The floral print reclining chair that fits me perfectly provides a comfortable place to curl up with a good book or to sneak in a short afternoon nap. Reading is one of my favorite pastimes. One shelf in the living area holds my small collection of colorful, leather bound books. I love the classics, and I read them over and over again. Since I don't retain what I read for very long, it all seems new again each time I open the cover.

Sentimental photo albums and picture frames adorn the antique mahogany coffee table. I love to peruse them frequently and share them with my visitors although names and faces escape me at times.

When Rose stops in every Thursday we talk about the good old days while the hours fly by. I always wish she could stay longer, but she will return next Thursday as promised. I can always count on Rose. She has never let me down.

But I feel like something is missing. It's hard to put my finger on it and even more difficult to understand what this feeling might mean. What I do know for sure is that things have not been the same since Alex left. The part of my heart that was filled with him is now empty. I remind myself that I just need to take one day at a time. I pray for guidance and courage. I miss the conversation and the companionship. I miss the security of having love right beside me. Is it wrong to want that back? Where on this heavenly earth could I find it? Is it even possible at my age? Is it fair to him or to his memory? I'm afraid and I'm confused.

* * *

My period of daydreaming was interrupted by a quiet rap on the door. I turned to look over my shoulder, raised my eyes and was surprised to see a familiar face. "Why, Rose! Is today Thursday? Please come in. I'm sorry. I just need two minutes to throw on some makeup." I place the photo album back on the coffee table and stood to give my guest a warm embrace. It's always a pleasure to spend time with Rose. We've remained close since our high school days and have pinkie-promised to always make time for each other.

It's almost noon and the two of us will be heading out for lunch as we do every Thursday. I stop at the mirror to put on my favorite pendant. It completes my appearance. It completes me.

We pass through the door and walk the short distance to the cozy café we visit regularly. We take our usual table which sets next to the always fresh salad bar. Iced teas are ordered and our conversation flows from one topic to another. The dining room seems busy once again today and the menu is familiar. I've noticed that most of the patrons are members of our generation, a few sporting hand-carved wooden canes, and a few more with varying stages of gray hair attempting to cover shiny bald spots. After all, it is noon on a Thursday when the younger generations are putting in a hard day's work and the children are attending school. I welcome the serene atmosphere.

As I observed the crowd, I momentarily met the eyes of a handsome gentleman who was sitting alone today. I was intrigued and simultaneously felt a passing flutter in my stomach. I guess I'm hungrier than I thought.

My focus returned to Rose and we munched away on chicken salad, fresh fruit and homemade bread pudding. It was good to catch up with Rose and what was happening in the outside community. I'm always amazed at the amount of news and gossip that occurred over the past week. Art Cavanaugh passed away on Tuesday. Died in his sleep they said, probable heart attack. Betsy Horn passed out in church again on Sunday. Took her into the hospital and put in one of those high-tech pacemakers. The newest redhead in town is Roxie Gates, but the color she left the salon with was more like a burnt orange, perfect if you were a fan of the Clemson Tigers. We just never seem to run out of things to talk about. The three hours we spent together seemed like three minutes.

Rose headed home to spend the rest of the day with Jonathan. This happily married couple is retired, Rose from the local high school where she served as the head cook for thirty-seven years and her husband from his accounting position with the Central Bank of Pennsylvania. They both seem to be in good health, although Jonathan did suffer a mild transient ischemic attack twelve years ago, but he made a full recovery and lives his life with no restrictions. Four of their grandchildren live nearby and keep their social calendar busy with numerous extracurricular activities to attend. Jonathan never discourages the time Rose spends with me.

* * *

I decided to forgo my afternoon siesta and forced myself to stop at the gym on my way back for a short workout. Dr. Powell and Alex always encouraged me to exercise frequently to maintain my strength and flexibility. They claimed the endorphins released during exertion were good for my brain.

My exercise regimen usually takes less than one hour. Not much to brag about, but it's better than nothing for this aging frame of mine. I enjoyed a short, leisurely stroll on the treadmill to warm up and wake up my muscles. Then I grabbed a yellow resistance band and challenged my flabby arms for a few repetitions followed by a brief ride on the stationary bike. Some relaxing stretches at the end and I was done. Someone's vision for a gym designed just for senior citizens was genius. We aren't intimidated by the young, toned, sculpted bodies that work harder, faster, stronger.

As I returned from a stop at the water fountain, I noticed across the room the gentleman from the café riding the recumbent bike. What a pleasing coincidence. He must be a member here too. Have I seen him here before? I'm not sure. I think I would remember such a good looking guy with those attractive blue eyes. I stole a glance as he was very easy to look at, and placed a mental picture in a corner of my mind. Our eyes met briefly as before, this time a shy thin smile appeared and he gave a nod of acknowledgment. Was he smiling at me? I felt the blood rush to my face and hoped he didn't notice. I couldn't prevent the awkward grin that appeared on my face and quickly turned away as that mysterious flutter returned to my stomach.

Chapter Nine

Rose will be here in twenty minutes. She is picking me up today for a planned trip downtown to do some Christmas shopping. We prefer the quaint little shops on the streets of Hanover as opposed to the hustle and bustle of the bigger cities. The retail owners here are friendly and have familiar faces, and the holiday bargains make the day worthwhile.

The storefronts may be overdone in the decorating department, but it sure makes for hours of enjoyable window shopping. The lampposts that line Main Street are adorned with Christmas wreaths accented with a perfectly tied bow. The hometown diners are busy all day serving breakfast, lunch and dinner to determined shoppers who are often caught humming familiar Christmas tunes. My favorite boutique, Angel's Attic, offers unique merchandise that often has a connection to the past. I rarely walk out the door without a shopping bag heavy with new purchases.

The Catholic Church near the center of town always displays a life-size nativity scene that is unmatched in its beauty. It comes to life on the last two weekends before Christmas when volunteer parishioners step in to replace the statues that stand in the snow. You may hear the voice of a cow or sheep that were brought in for the occasion from the Hobart farm.

Across the street, the fire station is the standard site for the popular visits from Santa Claus. The antique sleigh is decked out for the holiday and filled with small gifts that will be awarded to the children that come to convince Santa they've been good.

I'm almost ready. I look forward to this day-trip every year. I hurry and take a seat at the vanity to be sure I get my makeup just right. Sometimes I wonder why I bother. The wrinkles never seem to fade no matter how much nourishing cream I apply. My eyes are a little puffy today and it looks as if I have a second set of eyelids. At least I don't have a double chin to worry about. A little rose-shaded blush here and there. Lips are last; a little tint of gloss and I gently roll my lips together. A mist of finishing spray to my silver head of hair should just about do it.

Now to the dresser to select my jewelry for the event. Simple stud earrings will do. I don't want to distract any attention away from my favorite diamond pendant. I search for the black velvet box. I don't see it right away. I look again. Why isn't it here? I always put it in the same spot. I can't lose that pendant! It means the world to me. I begin to panic. My heart wants to jump out of my chest. Tears begin to fill the corners of my eyes until they spill over the edges and flow down my cheeks. I feel the color fade from my face and I suddenly feel nauseated. I've lost my spirit. I've lost my pendant! Saint Anthony, please help me!

At that moment, Rose arrives and notices my strain immediately. She queries, "Olivia, what is it? Tell me what's going on." I sputter rapidly with confusion as she tries to calm me. "It's the shopping. It's the jewelry." I'm pacing back and forth. My voice quivers. "It's the makeup. I can't find it. It's not here. It's the box. Where can it be?" I sit down as my strength abandons me. Rose gains some insight. "Is it your pendant, Olivia? You can't find your pendant?" I nod, unable to speak. She reassures me that it has to be here somewhere and she will turn over every corner of this room until she finds it.

She slowly and methodically searches every nook and cranny. Several tense minutes pass and I notice a sad look of concern on her face as she runs out of places to consider. Together we retrace the events of the last time I wore it, but nothing seems to shed any light for us. "We can't give up," Rose suggests. "Let's try to relax for a bit. We need time to think clearly. I'll pour us a half glass of wine."

I dry my tears, feeling a little better since Rose is there to help. "Thanks, Rose, the wine sounds good." She retrieves a bottle of white zinfandel from the refrigerator and returns with two wine glasses and a huge smile of relief. That seems odd. How can she smile at a time like this? She also holds in her hand a black velvet jewelry box. I nearly knocked her over as I suddenly regained my energy and jumped up to squeeze my friend who has found my treasure. "How did it get in there? Did I put it in there?" Rose pours the chilled wine and reassuringly says, "Now we can celebrate. All that matters is that we found your pendant." I agree, and sip with relief as Rose places the sparkling diamond around my neck. Now I am ready.

Chapter Ten

Once in a while I like to sleep in. Today is the day. My much needed beauty sleep was interrupted last night by some kind of commotion next door. Loud voices and people coming and going made it difficult to tune out the disturbing noises that continued throughout the night. I'll be sure to find some time to catch up on my sleep with a quick nap later this afternoon.

There is nothing scheduled to help pass the time today. Sometimes I welcome quiet days like this. Friends mean well by visiting or calling, but they don't understand that I don't need to be busy every minute of every day. You might often find me alone, but that doesn't necessarily mean that I am lonely.

Sipping my second cup of coffee flavored with French vanilla creamer, I continue to work the daily newspapers' simple crossword puzzle. Most days start with the same routine, but routine is good. Routine is familiar and makes me feel secure.

Before noon, I join three friendly neighbor ladies for a few challenging hands of bridge. Occasionally, a card or two may drop to the table or onto the tiled floor due to some numbness in the thin hands trying to hold them or the uncontrolled tremor that starts without warning. That brings shouts of "misdeal" and an accepted excuse to start again. No one is offended or in a hurry, after all, we have the entire day.

The game itself is good exercise for the mind, but the conversation is the most stimulating. We find ourselves often traveling back in time with sentences that begin with, "Remember when…?" We laugh and wonder what today's generation would think of black and white TV's, party telephone lines or humorous sitcoms like, I Love Lucy. Who could forget all of the sticky situations that Lucy, Ricky, Fred, and Ethel got into? The best episode in my opinion was called, Lucy Does a Television Commercial. Lucy was promoting a new health tonic called vitameatavegamin, which unknowingly contained a good dose of alcohol. Since the product name was a tongue twister for the sober person, you can imagine how difficult it became after more and more rehearsals were required. Lucy finishes in a hilarious state of inebriation that showcased her award-winning acting talent. Entertainment like this is sure hard to find in today's world.

The bridge group invited me to join them for lunch as we often do, but today I declined and retreated to my humble abode for some restful solitude. I selected one of my photo albums and positioned myself in my welcoming reclining chair. As I slowly turned the pages, I struggled to recall the story it was trying to tell. Advancing in years can be frustrating especially when you are trying to maintain memory, but the photos are helpful.

There's a picture of Alex and Max. My eyes close as I envision the two of them playing in the barnyard. The next page reveals my rose garden in all of its early summer glory. I can almost smell their sweet, familiar fragrance. The group of five men in the next photo is challenging me. I recognize Alex and his father, Charles, his brothers David and Gerald, but the third brother, what is his name? Why can't I think of it right now? This frustrates me once again. Resorting to my usual routine of proceeding through the alphabet from A to Z, I try to recall a familiar sounding letter. It's being stubborn and refused to come back to me. I take in a slow, deep breath and release it quickly in disappointment. Defeated, I carefully remove the photo from the clear plastic protector and turn it over to examine Alex's handwriting on the back. It's his brother Neil. Now I remember! "Neil, Neil, Neil," I repeat in hopes that it will stay in my head a little longer this time. Eyelids are heavy now, and I give in to a short break to rejuvenate myself.

* * *

A bolt of lightning strikes nearby and the immediate crack of thunder wake me with a start. The rain is coming down fairly hard, but the winds are calm. I rise to brew a cup of hot green tea for a late day pick-me-up. The novel I started reading yesterday beckons. It's another classic selected from the shelf, Jane Eyre. I love to read when it's softly raining. My goal is to try to read at least two chapters each day.

The evening TV schedule starts with an hour of local and national news followed by a variety of game shows with Jeopardy at the top of my list. On the rare occasion that I might answer correctly before the contestant does, I smile with pride.

When the sun nears the horizon, I complete my bedtime ritual of cleansing and moisturizing, brushing and flossing. The day's slacks and blouse are exchanged for a comfortable nightgown. Meditation and prayer fill the final minutes of every day, asking for health of mind, body and spirit, praising our heavenly Father and giving thanks for blessings received and answered prayers.

Chapter Eleven

The chef salad special at the café sounded like the perfect choice to satisfy my appetite today. Rose selected the baked spaghetti option with a small side salad. The aromas that drift from the gourmet kitchen here make your taste buds stand at attention. Meals served daily are always flavorful with little need for any additional seasoning. In the past, I was somewhat difficult to please when it came to the culinary arts. When a great dinner is one of the few social activities you have to look forward to, your expectations seem to rise and any disappointment is sadly frowned upon. My own success as a cook was well known in our small community, and I have to admit that I made the best pecan pie around.

As our plates are cleared from the table, we both agree to have a freshly perked cup of coffee. My mood is unusually dampened today and Rose takes notice. "Olivia, is something bothering you? You're awfully quiet today." I hesitate and wonder if she will understand. "I'm missing Alex a little more these days," as a heart-shaped tear slides down my rose powdered cheek. "I imagine him sitting here beside me. I wish I could reach out and touch him. Sometimes I sense that he is still with me or perhaps within me. It's just so hard to explain." Rose places her warm hand on top of mine. "He is always near you, Olivia. You have to believe that." I take in a long, deep breath trying to compose myself and catch the tear in my linen napkin. "I do, Rose."

My heart skipped a beat when I saw him. The familiar male figure slowly and gingerly stood and positioned his wheeled walker in front of him. I watch with a concerned stare. I recognize the signs of pain in his eyes and in his posture, but he is determined in his effort. He shares parting words with the others at his table and walks toward the exit which will lead him directly past us. My heart rate accelerates and my palms become moist. The air goes in and out of my lungs more quickly now. I wring the napkin that lies in my lap. The contents of my stomach are churning more than usual. These feelings are strange to me in a way, yet familiar in that I have felt them in the past, perhaps fifty years ago.

The anticipation is building as he approaches ever nearer. It seems I can't take my eyes off of him. Shall I speak to him? I want to. What would I say? I feel like a shy school girl for some reason. Too many thoughts, too many memories, too many emotions are flooding my brain. In all the confusion I decide to maintain my silence. He is even closer now and he pauses beside us. "Hello, Rose. Hello, Olivia." He hesitates for a moment as if he wanted to say more but changed his mind and continued on by.

I looked down at my empty coffee cup then up at my friend Rose. She had an inquisitive look in her eyes as she noticed my unease yet said nothing. I know she must be trying to process what's going on in my mind. It would be a blessing if she can figure it out because I certainly don't understand it. After a few moments of silence, a calmness returns to my body. Rose speaks softly with a smile, "Why, Olivia, I do believe you are blushing!" I was never one to disguise my feelings, especially from my closest friend who knows me through and through. We both smile and giggle like two love-crazy teenagers sharing intimate secrets. My fluctuating mood has suddenly changed to new and improved. "He knows my name, Rose. He knows my name!" I don't know what I am feeling right now, but I think I like it!

Chapter Twelve

Today I sit alone on the outdoor terrace soaking up some early morning sun. The nearby flower pots have been watered by last evening's welcomed shower. The multi-colored fall mums have sprung to life following their refreshing drink. I like to sit here to relax, to be alone with my thoughts, to pray. There's a little chill in the air and my blue sweater feels good on my shoulders. I try to plan the rest of my day, but my thoughts are unsettled so I continue to sit and meditate. I should go to the gym, but my body tells me "no". I'm feeling a little sluggish for some reason. My sleep patterns are changing and last night was not a restful one. An afternoon nap sounds like a good possibility.

It seems my days are often the same. One day is the mirror image of the day before and the hands on the clock move slowly. I'm longing for something new. I'm longing for someone new, and I have an eerie feeling that I might know who he is.

My peaceful quiet has been interrupted by the sound of a well-used walker rolling over the red patio pavers. The kind looking gentleman with a familiar smile sits in the chair next to me and gently rocks back and forth in a soothing rhythm. My heart begins to warm. His eyes turn in my direction and he speaks first, "Nice morning isn't it?" I hesitate as I try to collect my thoughts. I decide not to let this moment pass me by and I nervously respond, "Yes it is. I'm enjoying it." I take in a deep breath to try to relax. I think *just be yourself*, but I'm not sure who that is anymore. A few awkward minutes pass in silence.

He sure is handsome for an older man. A good amount of hair still covers his head and the so called crow's feet have left a permanent mark in the usual places. His hands are calloused and strong which tells me he was a good, hard worker. That might explain the stiffness that is now apparent in the movement of his body.

The small talk continued as we learned that our pasts held a lot in common. I began to feel more at ease. I discovered that he lives nearby which makes the option of meeting again a real possibility that I look forward to. He discovered that I am slow to trust and realizes he must be patient and take one small step at a time.

Before we part, he proposes an offer. "Olivia, I would like to see you again. Would you join me for lunch tomorrow?" Surprisingly, I don't hesitate with my reply. "Of course, I would love to." His eyes brighten as he appeared to get the answer he was hoping for. We agree to meet at our favorite café that is in a convenient location for both of us. Noon tomorrow can't get here soon enough. I'm excited for it. I'm happy. I have to tell Rose!

She answers the phone after the third ring and sounds glad to hear my voice. "Rose, you are not going to believe this. I have a date! Imagine that, at my age! Am I crazy or what?" I can sense her smiling on the other end of the line. I explain the details of my eventful morning and she instinctively knows who I am talking about. She is genuinely happy for me and tells me so. I ask if I am doing the right thing as a nagging doubt sets in. Rose will be honest with me. Is it right? What would be wrong with wanting a new friend, a companion, someone to spend time with? What's wrong with not wanting to be alone? What's wrong with having something to look forward to? I realize I'm trying to justify the idea in my own mind. Rose is on my side. She has always given me good advice. She encourages me to live my life with no regrets. I pause to ponder the scenarios. I have a strange feeling that for some reason, this was meant to be. A second chance at love.

* * *

I have an hour to get ready for my date. I was up before the sun this morning anticipating a wonderful day. Rose called to wish me luck and told me to enjoy myself. She made me promise to call her later today to fill her in on all the juicy details. Some things never change. I giggle at the thought. I'm pretty sure there's not going to be anything juicy going on at our age.

Looking out the window, I notice an icy rain pounding the panes of glass. The weatherman is predicting a change to snow in a couple of hours. I refuse to let what's happening outside dampen what will be happening inside today.

The dress I've selected is one of my favorites. It's a belted a-line dress in a shade of teal blue with a long matching cardigan. It complements my thin figure and my skin tone. I apply a new coat of clear acrylic polish to my brittle nails. The smiling reflection in the mirror confirms that my hair and makeup are satisfactory.

My excitement begins to build and it's time to leave for

our rendezvous. Fear of possible rejection clouds my thoughts again. What if he doesn't come? What would it feel like to be stood up? What if he comes but decides he's not interested in pursuing a relationship? What if I feel the same?

The short walk to the café gives me little time to collect my thoughts. Shyly I enter and nervously scan the empty tables. My peripheral vision senses movement to my left. Turning in that direction, he comes into focus. His eyes pull me in and I notice he is wearing a crisp dress shirt and tie, and a pleasant expression. Feelings of doubt are instantly replaced by hopeful anticipation as I smile and approach the table. This mannered gentleman rises to greet me and slowly pulls out my chair as he waits for me to be seated. We exchange hellos and I notice a single long-stemmed rose in the center of the table. The deep crimson petals are perfectly formed and the sweet fragrance is enjoyable. "It's for you, Olivia," he says. "I hope you like it." My heart is happy. "I certainly do. Thank you." Our eyes connect briefly then return to scan the menu. We make our selections and relay our order to the waitress. We start to exchange questions and answers, and share memories of our pasts and hopes for what's left of our future. He holds my attention and I feel like we are in our own little world oblivious to others around us. Nothing else matters at this moment. It feels like the sands of time are standing still. I feel calm, relaxed and lost in time. Maybe I feel a connection.

We frequently laugh as he cheerfully tells jokes about politics and old age. He is very entertaining and the clock on the wall indicates we have been here nearly two hours. We agree that we have been sitting far too long and need to get up and move to restore our circulation. Reluctantly, we walk toward the door and I stop dead in my tracks. "Please wait here."

I hurried back to the table for the glass vase that holds my beautiful rose. Returning to him to discuss our departure, I have a good feeling about today and I thank him again for the rose and an amazing time. He nods with similar thoughts and politely asks if he can stroll with me. Overjoyed, I consent and we slowly walk around the corner to my place.

When I open the door, I invite him in for some continued conversation. The vase from the café is placed on the coffee table and I feel him watching my every move. He notices the photos there and asks permission to take a look. Why would I object? Anything that enables me to spend more time with this fine man is a good thing. He seems uneasy when he focuses on one photo in particular. The bride and groom posing in front of the church on a wintry day look so happy. Turning toward me and waiting for me to comment, he only sees me shrug my shoulders in mystery with a glum look on my face. I say nothing.

Discussion is quickly diverted to a recap of today's pleasure and promises to pursue more possibilities. Careful not to wear out his welcome, he walks to the door. He slowly leans over the walker and reaches for my hands to pull me closer. I tremble inside anticipating his next move. Is he going to kiss me? Do I want him to? What will it feel like? Will I enjoy it? Will he?

With my left hand in his right, he gently strengthens his grip and raises my trembling hand to his lips. His welcoming flesh meets mine as he places a sweet, tender kiss there. My face warms with the color of a blush. His eyes twinkle with satisfaction as we share this innocent joy; a loving memory that I hope will not fade as some of the others have.

Our shared space now widens and he moves through the

door as I watch until he disappears around the corner. The expression on my face just might be a permanent smile.

* * *

Sweet dreams filled my restful night. Thoughts of the emotional day lured me to sleep like a lullaby. I didn't want to wake up. As the first light of day illuminates my room, I wonder if he will call me. Glancing at my phone, waiting for it to vibrate reminds me that I had forgotten something. Rose! I forgot to call Rose last night! How could I forget? I was all wrapped up in my own little world I guess, but that's no excuse for my lack of consideration.

I jump from bed and dial her ten digit number as fast as my arthritic fingers will let me. It's not too early to call. Rose and Jonathan have always gotten up with the chickens. I'm just hoping she can forgive me and I take a deep breath as she answers immediately. "It's me, Rose. I'm sorry I didn't call last night. I have no excuse." Pouring a glass of orange juice I wait for her reaction. "Never mind that, dearie, tell me about your date!" Hearing the excitement in her voice, I describe every moment in amazing detail and hope I'm painting her the picture accurately.

Confessing my feelings is easy, understanding them is the hard part. Rose listens, responds, and listens some more as I excitedly ramble on. When the story is complete, I ask for her opinion. "Olivia, I like what I am hearing. There is nothing wrong with what you are feeling. I'm happy for you and I hope you see him again." I am relieved and thankful for my kind and patient friend. We make plans to do lunch again soon.

Later, my phone rings and a deep, smooth voice begins a

heartwarming conversation.

We scheduled a second date in three days, and eventually continued meeting on a weekly basis. Time was spent sharing dinners, playing cards, joining in a bingo game or simply watching a classic movie. I was happier than I had been in years. We both found a new energy we didn't know existed. Something special was happening and it felt good.

* * *

Christmas was only a week away as we sat discussing how we wanted to spend this special holiday together. The shopping and wrapping was done. I mailed my short stack of cards yesterday. The table-top tree was trimmed. A white Christmas was doubtful due to an untimely rain and a slow moving warm-front predicted to last several more days.

We just finished watching, A Christmas Story, laughing at the usual scenes when Alex suddenly became quiet as a mouse. I wish I could read his mind. He looked deeply into my eyes, "I want to ask you something, and I want you to think about it carefully before you answer." I'm confused by his seriousness and meekly nod for him to continue. Slowly, the words come. "Olivia, may I please take you to midnight mass? It would mean the world to me." He nervously waits for my decision. I realize how I have missed this tradition from the past. I'm not sure why I haven't been to church lately, but Christmas Eve seemed an appropriate time to return and ask for forgiveness. "Yes, I would be happy to go with you." He closed his eyes in thanks and grins widely as he opens them. "I promise you, it will be a night to remember." I'm thrilled with our plans, but I mysteriously wonder what he meant by that.

Chapter Thirteen

Christmas carols are playing on the radio, and it took me a few seconds to realize I was singing along. Soon I will be sharing Christmas Eve dinner with Rose and Jonathan before midnight mass. They always welcome me warmly into their home not only over the holidays, but all year long. Rose loves spending time in the kitchen, and dinner is sure to be something special. I'm wearing my new ivory Christmas sweater that is the perfect background for my blue diamond pendant.

A light mist is falling when Jonathan arrives. He offered to pick me up while Rose is busy putting the finishing touches on our dinner. I grab my purse and two wrapped gifts and take Jonathan's arm. Why is he stopping? He looks disappointed. "Olivia, aren't you going to wear a coat? You'll be sure to catch cold if you don't." It took a little bit for my brain waves to transmit. I reverse my steps and retrieve my winter coat from the nearby closet. Embarrassed, I struggle to hold back the tears. *For heaven's sake, Olivia, don't let Jonathan see you cry. It's Christmas Eve!* He didn't seem to notice, and the negative feelings pass. My fluctuating mood must improve, and promptly at that. Quickly, we dodge the raindrops and are finally on our way.

Rose squeezes me hard when I walk through the door and

expresses her sincere happiness for the exciting new changes in my life. I thank her for the kind remarks then follow my nose to the kitchen.

A cherry pie with lattice crust sits on the counter waiting for its after-dinner debut. When I turn on the oven light, I can tell that the stuffed, golden brown turkey is almost done. The drippings that have collected in the pan will be used to make Rose's delicious lump-free gravy. Potatoes are gently boiling on the stove and hazelnut coffee is perking. Cranberry jello salad complete with apples, celery and nuts is chilling in the refrigerator. The table is set with Rose's grandmother's china, crystal wine goblets and recently polished silverware. A bottle of champagne is propped up in the ice bucket waiting to be uncorked. The cook calls her guests to the table. "Dinner is served. Let us give thanks."

Rose's hard work is a complete success as always. Taste buds are pleased and stomachs are full. We move toward the twinkling Christmas tree to exchange our simple gifts. Fortunes are not spent here but the sentiments are priceless. Rose insists her guest come first so I open a dainty wooden music box that plays a soothing tune, The Way We Were. Recalling the first line of the lyrics, I hum along. Jonathan unwraps his gift - a new book to add to his collection on the Civil War and he immediately starts flipping the pages. Rose carefully pulls the white bow off of her small gift box. The prize inside produces a grateful smile. An antique cameo broach in soft shades of ivory and rose is removed and immediately pinned to her red Christmas sweater. Heartfelt hugs are exchanged and wine glasses are emptied. The evening has been wonderful so far.

The doorbell interrupts our conversation and Jonathan greets the man who is waiting to escort me to midnight mass.

"We must hurry," he says, "if we want to hear the choir sing." I thank my hosts for an amazing time and we wish them "Merry Christmas". I remember my coat this time and join him under the umbrella as we head to the car. The temperature is dropping a few degrees and the cold rain is changing to a light, wet snow that melts immediately when it reaches the warmer earth.

The church bells are ringing familiar hymns as we enter. Rolling down the aisle we chose an empty pew on the right. Scanning the familiar church I admire how beautifully it is decorated and I am glad to be back. Prayers that I can still remember are recited silently in my head and I thank The Lord for this night and for this compassionate man who has come into my life. I reach for his hand and interlace my fingers with his. They fit together perfectly and we scoot a little closer.

The choir sounds angelic as flutes, trumpets and drums softly chime in. The mass is moving and the sermon is pleasingly short. Young, exhausted children have fallen asleep in their parent's arms. The recessional hymn of, Joy to the World, concludes and I rise to leave. He pulls me to him and asks me to sit for awhile. The parishioners file out and shouts of astonishment at a new fallen snow could be heard. It seems we've been gifted with a white Christmas after all.

Finally, we are alone. When the soft organ music quiets, we exit the pew and he leads me toward the sacristy. There we pause at the nativity scene that distinctly reminds us what this night is about. We stand hand-in-hand surrounded by a graceful silence. I wouldn't want to be anywhere else at this moment or with anyone else for that matter. He looks down at me lovingly, waiting for me to say something, but I am lost in my thoughts and remain silent. He starts to speak,

"Remember when we..." Suddenly and awkwardly he stops mid-sentence, closes his eyes and bows his head. His breathing becomes quick and shallow. He's holding something back, but what? Perhaps if I put my arms around him it would encourage him to go on. I meekly slip one arm around his waist, then the other and move my palms up to rest upon his shoulder blades. He responds by wrapping both arms around me and pulls me closer. I feel safe. I feel content. I feel loved.

My heart pounds rapidly once again as I lay my head on his chest and I can clearly hear his heart pounding too. My fragile emotions are flowing like the mighty Mississippi and my knobby knees are weak. I haven't felt this way since my wedding day. He pulls away, but only slightly so he can look into my eyes. He tenderly caresses my face in his hands and leans in. I close my hazel-green eyes and feel like I am floating without gravity. I can sense his lips moving ever nearer and he gently places a warm, loving kiss on the tip of my nose. "I love you, Livy," he whispers.

My watery eyes open with a start as I undergo a moment of déjà vu. Taking a quick step back, I look into those deep-set baby blue eyes and notice the moisture that surrounds them. Words escape me, but I am able to force an uneasy hint of a smile. My brow furrows. He nonchalantly reaches his right hand into his pocket and produces what appears to be an old photograph. He unfolds it carefully and hands it to me. It is worn and faded. I give it a lengthy stare through eyes that are suddenly filling. Something stirs in my heart and in my mind. Could it be that I've seen this photo before?

Suddenly, a disturbing connection flashes through me and electrifies my heart as it begins to pound even harder. Is it the same bride and groom that sit among the photos on my coffee table? I instantly gasp. My hands fly to my mouth in disbelief as the photo floats to the floor. The room is spinning. The blood quickly drains from my face. I feel lightheaded and break into a sweat. I need to sit down, now! Alex?

Chapter Fourteen

I'm worried about Olivia. I need to talk to Alex again. I've shared my concerns with Jonathan and he agrees that this is something we just can't ignore and hope that it will go away. The subtle changes I've noticed seem to be progressing the way Alex explained they would. He gets good information from Dr. Powell and from the support group he attends. He also reads every book he can get his hands on about this mystifying disease. Her body seems strong as she has been blessed with generally good health, but her mind is unpredictable.

The conversations we have are growing shorter and she has difficulty staying focused. Her expression is often blank and I wonder what she is thinking if anything at all. Recall of the events of long ago remains accurate, but it's disheartening to discover that she isn't sure what day it is or that she can't remember what she had for lunch twenty-four hours ago. Olivia cares less about her appearance these days which is way out of character for this once proud woman who in the past made sure every strand of hair was in place before she stepped out the door.

During our last visit, I noticed the photos on her coffee table were missing. She told me she had to put them away. She didn't like strangers watching her. I mysteriously wonder, am I a stranger too? I can't bear the thought. Even though she welcomed me in, it dawned on me that she did not call me by name. I whisper to myself, "Olivia, please come back. I need you."

What about Alex? He has certainly suffered in silence. Always present by her side every step of the way. He has shown us all what true love really means. Alex never gives up on anything and that includes trying to bring her memory back. Going to her room every morning religiously to remind her what day it was, to take her medication and to get dressed. Showing her the photos again and again, naming the people who were captured there. He talked to Olivia about their life together but he felt like she wasn't really listening. To her, it was someone else's story. He never gave up hope that maybe today he will say or do the one thing that would bring her back to him. He dreams of nothing else.

Olivia eventually began to feel uncomfortable with his presence. She would put more distance between them as he struggled to bring them closer. She seemed afraid that he might reach out to touch her. Alex achingly longed for her touch. She would sit in silence with no response to the conversation he wanted to have with her. Her confused expression and frequent irritability forced Alex to rethink his plan. After all, he didn't want to do anything to hurt Olivia. The last thing he needed was to make her unhappy. With a heavy heart he made a difficult decision to lessen the contact with this wife, but would always watch her from a distance. He will watch over her forever. It was heartbreaking to watch him try to reach out to her under these trying circumstances.

* * *

As he drove to Rose and Jonathan's for dinner, the headlights illuminated the light snow that was falling and Alex noticed how big the flakes were getting. He thought of Olivia and remembered a time when they were dating. It was the night of the final home football game. Our team had won, pulling off a victory in the final seconds putting everyone in a celebratory mood. As the fans dispersed, he warmed Olivia's hand in his as they made their way back to her house leaving footprints in the snow. She would laugh and blink as the snowflakes tickled her lashes. They ran and jumped in an effort to snatch the largest flake on their tongues. It was innocent and fun. It was memorable. Alex knew at this moment that she would be watching the new fallen snow from her bay window and he wondered if that memory was still there for her?

* * *

During the flavorful pot roast supper and apple crumb pie with ice cream dessert, the discussion centered on our concerns about Olivia. The three of us tried to accept what was happening. The cross we are all carrying is getting heavier now and we need to consider the future. Jonathan and I worry about Alex too, but he remains strong and encourages us not to give up. I don't know how he does it. There's no quit of any kind among the men who bear the Rousch family name. He continues to have a positive attitude but deep down he knows he is losing her as her memory slips away a little more. He is resilient. He is devoted and faithful to his vows of matrimony. He is love's hero. He is not broken...yet.

Chapter Fifteen

I lost my wife, my best friend eight years ago. The disease that is slowly taking her away from me has no cure according to Dr. Powell. 'It is treatable, Alex, but it will continue to progress until her body can no longer fight back'. The news was devastating but it brought some understanding to what was happening between us. The support group I attended helped me realize that I cannot attempt to read her mind without misunderstanding what was hiding in the corners there, that I can't expect to understand meaningful words that often went unspoken, and that I would know the right time when my own silence was necessary.

The vow I made to myself and to my Livy was to make sure we both had a reason to look forward to each new day. To feel contentment and trust. To make sure she felt loved, and every day find a way to keep her memory alive. It consumes me. I will never give up.

Our marriage of fifty-six years was tested in many small ways, but none as monumental or as challenging as this. 'For better or for worse, in sickness and in health' keeps playing in my mind like a broken record. I was determined to provide for Olivia for as long as I was physically able. I wanted it to be forever. But the deteriorating effects of osteoarthritis caused my weakening body to fail me. My personal safety and mobility became an issue that made caring for myself nearly impossible, much less being responsible for the care and safety of another.

With a heavy heart and dwindling hope, the time had come to consider our long term care options. It was hard to accept the fact that our circumstances now required us to depend on strangers for our day-to-day needs, rather than each other. Grudgingly I traveled from place to place covering three nearby counties to take the informative tours and attentively listen to the sales pitches and weigh our options.

After many long days and longer nights, the decision was made to settle into Rosewood Senior Living. It had a nice location just outside of Hanover. The choice to stay close to home felt like the right one. I was content to know that our established church, family and friends were not going to change even though our home would.

They accepted Olivia into the memory care unit where specially trained personnel would give her the best care possible. I would be located in a nearby wing for the assisted living residents. We could share in all of the facility's numerous activities and social events and could even share the same dining room if we so desired. They had a well-equipped exercise room we would both enjoy using. We also had the option to leave the campus on field trips or private excursions with the staff's approval.

My room was pretty standard, and that was fine with me. My heart really wasn't into it anyway. At times I feel like I have failed in keeping my promises to Livy. "Please forgive me, sweetheart, and I will work on trying to forgive myself."

Olivia's room was more suitable for a woman. It had a

large bay window with one of the best views on campus and she deserved it. I tried to surround her with some of her favorite things to make her feel more at home. Her most treasured items being the numerous photo albums that tell our story, and the sentimental picture frames carefully placed on the mahogany coffee table. I continue to hope that someday those moments stored on black and white photo paper will by chance bring her memory back to life.

Jonathan and Rose had promised to stand by us the day they were witnesses at our wedding and they have not failed. Our inseparable foursome that formed so many years ago has managed to stick together like glue. None of us could have imagined that we would face such an unfair crisis down the road. We have aged gracefully and are lucky to have outlived others younger than us. I have depended on them when needed, but was careful not to overburden them with the trials and tribulations that were my own.

Our old friends were the first to notice the ill effects these past eight years were having on me and they were concerned. I felt I had coped pretty well and tried to listen to other's advice and also manage to take care of myself. If only there had been one small step forward, one encouraging sign of improvement, one glimmer of hope to inspire me, to renew me, to keep the fight in me alive. But there was none. I looked for it. I imagined it. I dreamed of it.

Reality has finally set in. It came to me as I prayed. God said, "Well done, Alexander Rousch. Now seek the peace you have denied yourself." I fear the time has come to wise up, accept the inevitable and prepare for a peaceful conclusion. My desperate efforts to revive Olivia's mind and memory have failed. The terminal disease has won. My fragile body is tired and I feel like I am falling to pieces. I have lost my strength. I have finally lost hope. My tender heart is breaking.

Life with Olivia has been a remarkable blessing for which I am grateful. Our marriage survived the test of time and we were perfect together. My wavering faith has been tested as I frequently wonder why it has to end this way, but I hold onto the promise of a heavenly world and truly believe that it does exist. I live for the end of the present and look forward to the future.

The sun is setting ever so slowly on our life and on our love. It is beautiful, breathtaking and full of color. It is peaceful. It is memorable. I promise not to let go of the love we endlessly share. 'Till death do us part'. We are devoted until eternity and then some.

When the sun was finally gone, all that remained was darkness.

# # #

A Simple Strand of Twinkle Lights

NICK

By: Jan Romes

Chapter One

Nick Barstow scowled into the hallway mirror on his way out the door. Not exactly the expression of choice; but hey, he'd flipped the calendar from November to December, and the frown automatically fell into place – just like it had done for the last two years. Whether he liked it or not, it would stay until New Year's.

Charging down the front steps of his apartment building, he almost knocked over Midge Pennington, the quirky, grey-haired lady who lived next to him. Nick caught Midge and the two sacks of groceries she was toting before they fell. "Sorry, Midge, I was preoccupied and didn't see you. Are you okay?"

"I am now." She blinked up and pretended to swoon.

Nick playfully rolled his eyes. Midge was in her late seventies, could make pie like she owned a bakery, and had watched Francine Vanguard dump him on the very stoop they stood on. Since then, Midge tried to nurture his wounds with pie and flirting. The flirting was a form of high-grade duct tape meant to hold his heart together.

Midge's aged blue eyes glistened. "My granddaughter is coming."

"That's nice." Nick glanced at his watch. Happy-hour

started at four, and it was already three-thirty. His patrons could wait an extra five or ten minutes to *get happy*, but he really needed to get moving. First, he had to help Midge.

He slid Midge's over-sized purse back onto her shoulder and hefted the sacks of groceries from her hands. "Lead the way, sweetheart."

"Aww, Nick, you're such a gentleman." She winked. "Did I mention my granddaughter is coming?"

"Yep." Either Midge was getting senile or she had something up her sleeve. Knowing Midge, it was the latter. To save time, he should just ask. Asking his feisty neighbor anything usually resulted in a thirty-minute answer that included a pot of coffee and slice of coconut cream pie. Tempting. But not today. Besides, she'd lecture him about the scowl.

Midge's gnarled fingers made it difficult to get the key in the lock. Nick would happily set the groceries down to help, but the old gal had a stubborn streak as big as her heart. She was determined not to succumb to the symptoms of age. Finally, a click said she showed the key and lock who was boss. She latched onto Nick's arm and guided him inside.

Nick deposited the groceries on the counter and turned to leave. "It was good to see you, Midge."

"Not so fast." Her expression lit up like Christmas. "I forgot to tell you, my granddaughter…"

"I know," he tweaked her chin with his thumb and forced a smile to hide his impatience, "your granddaughter is coming."

"Macy's going to stay with me for awhile." Midge leaned in like she was sharing a secret. "That ratfink ex-husband of hers pressured the poor girl into selling the house so he could get his half of the money. If I run into him, I'm going to karate chop his neck."

There's no doubt the spirited old gal would give the guy his comeuppance. Midge was short in stature so Nick would have to lift her up to get to the guys' neck. Since his lifting-services weren't needed right now, he had to go. He took another step toward the door.

Midge cut in front of him with a toothy smile. "Macy could use a job, Nick." Her grin faded into grandmotherly concern.

While Nick didn't experience the sting of having to divide personal property with Francine since they never made it to the altar, he still understood what Midge's granddaughter was dealing with. He also understood Midge's inclination to fix things. But he wasn't thrilled to take on a new employee. As the sole owner and lone employee of the bar, he didn't have to trip over anyone's schedule but his own. He liked it that way. Midge's pleading blue eyes said that was about to change. If he didn't hire Macy, she would karate chop his neck too. "Does she have any barmaid experience?"

"None whatsoever," Midge spouted like it was no big deal. "She kept the books for the ratfink's plumbing business."

"What makes you think she'd want to work for me? I mean, it's a bar. Lots of alcohol. Listening to people share their troubles. The occasional rowdy drunk. Not the best place to heal a broken heart." He knew first-hand it wasn't a good place to mend. When Francine ditched him for a guy who promised to whisk her away to the French Alps for Christmas – a guy she met while working in his bar – it had been a real test to listen to customers bellyache about their day when his sucked. Two years later, it was still a test.

"A bar is exactly what she needs. Lots of music and noisy

customers to drown out her thoughts." Before Nick could say that it didn't work for him, she continued. "Besides, she's been a homebody for far too long. She needs to mingle with the real world, and you can't get any more real than a bar."

It was hard to argue with Midge, so he didn't. "Tell her to stop by to fill out an application."

Midge's eyes shimmered with accomplishment and something else he couldn't quite pin down. "You're a great guy, Nick." She patted him on the back. "Macy will drop by later. And please, don't scare her off with that grouchy look, okay?"

* * *

Macy Kincade took a hesitant step into Barstow's Tavern. Expecting to find a dark, dingy establishment thick with the stench of spilled beer and greasy food, she was surprised to find the opposite. Semi-closed wooden shutters streamed in enough sunlight to keep things from looking murky. The scent of pine gave it a fresh-scrubbed smell. It was a small place with padded booths and round tables. An L-shaped bar was decked out with worn, but well-kept bar stools. A mirrored-wall behind the bar was accompanied by neon beer signs, shelves of liquor, and an engraved wooden plaque that read, 'Barstow's Tavern est. 2008'. In the far corner she spotted a pool table and dart board.

Not bad. She could work there.

Someone's cell phone rang to the tune of Jingle Bells. The music made Macy realize it was the only thing in Barstow's that hinted it was Christmastime. All the other businesses up and down the street were decorated to the hilt, but the bar didn't have as much as a string of twinkle lights anywhere.

Her gaze skipped around looking for the guy who fit her grandmother's description – dark hair, brown eyes, face stubble, and a permanent scowl. She found him bussing a table in the corner, his hands filled with empty long-neck beer bottles. "Mr. Barstow?"

"Yes?" One of the beer bottles was close to escaping his grasp.

Macy's brain must've tilted sideways. Instead of taking the bottle, she pushed it up so he wouldn't lose it. Huge blunder. The half dozen or so bottles went from his hands to the floor.

Angry brown eyes raked Macy. "What was that?"

She took a step back. "I tried to help."

Nick bumped his brows together even tighter than they already were, shook his head, and heavy-footed it to the kitchen. He returned with a broom and dust pan. Macy stepped out of the way while he swept up the shattered bits of glass. "Did you need something?"

Yes, for the air to return to her lungs. It took a few seconds to resume breathing and to find her voice. "I wanted to fill out an application." Her grandmother warned that Nick Barstow could slice and dice her with just a look. At the moment, his brown-eyed slicer was hard at work. She shifted from foot to foot.

Someone seated at the bar hollered for a beer. Someone else added that they were in dire need of a margarita. The bells above the door signaled the arrival of more customers, bringing the place to near full-capacity. It appeared that Nick needed to be cloned. "I'm kind of busy right now," he said stiffly.

"Let me help. Hire me."

Nick's harsh glare dropped to the mess.

Macy squared her shoulders. "That was a one-time thing.

It won't happen again." A lift of his eyebrow said he wasn't convinced.

A customer eager to partake in happy-hour called his name. "Come on, Nick, I want to pound a few before I have to go home to the wife."

Nick expelled a long breath. Macy bravely placed her hands on the broom. "I'll get this. Go help your customers."

He studied her for a few long seconds and relinquished the broom. "Be careful."

Macy sighed. Her fresh start had already met a jagged path of resistance.

* * *

Nick filled a frosty mug with draught beer and watched the short-haired, twenty-something blonde with amazing blue eyes tackle the mess then move on to clear an adjacent table. He hadn't caught her name but she had to be Macy. The music floating from the jukebox managed to drown out his grunt of displeasure. Regardless of what he'd said to Midge earlier, he couldn't hire her granddaughter. She looked too much like…

"Barstow, are you going to bring me that beer fairly soon, or wait until the frost melts off the mug?" Jim Simmons heckled from the end of the bar.

Jim was one of Nick's best customers. He worked in the bank down the street and generally lingered at the tavern until closing time. Nick and Jim became buddies and were friendly rivals when it came to football. Nick rooted for the Jets. Jim supported the Giants. They trashed-talked and placed an occasional bet. "Bite me, Simmons."

Nick delivered the beer and it was half-gone in one gulp. Jim smacked his lips and nodded toward Macy. "Who's the cute little number with the broom?"

Nick winced. He seriously didn't want to hire Macy, but sometimes a guy had to suck it up and do the right thing. He groaned without making a sound. "My new barmaid."

Jim's eyes filled with mischief. "You lucky, S.O.B.!"

S.O.B was true enough. The lucky part remained to be seen. Macy was clumsy and a mirror-image of Francine. Actually, Macy was shorter and had a better smile. "Whatever." Nick wandered off to wash a few empty mugs. He aimed his gaze at Macy. Instead of cleaning the mugs, he dropped them into a plastic dish tub. In spite of the unrest building inside, he folded an application in half and stuffed it in his back pocket.

Macy had climbed into the booth to wipe down the far end of the table, when Nick approached she flinched but smiled. Nick couldn't stop a portion of his scowl from slipping away. He slid into the seat across from her. "You're Macy," he stated matter-of-factly.

She nodded and stretched her hand across the table for a handshake.

Nick eyed the delicate hand before taking it. He lifted is gaze to connect with Macy's. Her blue eyes made him zero in closer. Those were not Francine's eyes. Not even close. His heart did a strange jangle in his chest. He gave her hand a swift shake, cleared his throat and laid the application on the table. "This is just a formality. The job is yours." He pointed to two spots on the form. "All you have to fill out is your full name and social security number. I know where you'll be living and Midge has vouched for you so I don't need references." He would probably regret hiring her, one more thing he could add to an already heaping list.

"I can't thank you enough, Nick."

Her warm, soft voice chipped away even more of the scowl. Dammit all to hell.

* * *

Macy was stunned by the charge of electricity that raced through her body when Nick touched her hand. She'd read about that happening in books but never in her wildest dreams did she think it could actually happen. She swallowed hard and studied the serious brown eyes that were studying her too. "I know you don't have time to show me the ropes right now." She gestured to the crowd that seemed momentarily satisfied. "I'd be happy to hang around until closing time so you could teach me."

"Sounds like a plan." Nick scooted from the booth. "Can you cook?"

"According to my ex, I can't." Ack! Macy didn't mean to cloud the conversation by mentioning the rodent who mucked up four years of her life. Nick's expression returned to the severe scowl from moments ago and she attempted to lighten things back up. "Your customers won't have to have their stomachs pumped." She laughed. He didn't.

"I serve a limited menu – burgers, chicken strips, fries, coleslaw and chef salads. If you could make a few chef salads up ahead, that would be great." Nick walked away without further instruction and blended in with the crowd.

Macy had a feeling that Nick Barstow's good looks but dismal temperament would make working for him a challenge. Although, she was amazed at the powerful pull of his eyes and how her own eyes kept drifting to his mouth, wondering how he kissed. A long whoosh of reality gushed from somewhere close to her soul. For reasons she couldn't understand, she navigated to great looking guys with foul dispositions. Her ex was easy on the eyes but had the personality of a rabid badger. Nick Barstow was fine to look at but his constant frown warned of trouble ahead, plus he had the patience of a gnat. Thank God this job was temporary. If… She shook her head. *When* she found permanent employment in an office, she'd be out of his hair; hopefully before their relationship became as toxic as the one she had with the ratfink.

Macy wandered to the kitchen. It was a tiny space with stainless steel counters perfect for assembling salads. She found lettuce, tomatoes, hard boiled eggs, and packages of ham, chicken, and turkey in the walk-in cooler. A search in the cabinets above the counter produced real dishes, and a smile. There were no foam plates or cups, and no plastic cutlery anywhere. Nick walked in just as she said, "Way to go, Nick."

"For what?"

She blushed at having been caught talking to herself. "For being environmentally- friendly." She pointed to the ceramic bowls she was using for the chef salads.

Nick blew off the compliment. "The disposable stuff isn't cost effective." He wiped his hands on a bar towel and stood there for a second, like he was going to say more on the subject. When he turned to drop a basketful of fries into the fryer she knew he changed his mind. "I'll be back in a couple of minutes to get those."

Macy sighed. Nick Barstow was a puzzle. One minute he appeared to thaw, the next he turned into a polar ice cap. And she had no idea what triggered either one.

Snowflakes the size of quarters fell past the only window in the kitchen. Macy loved snow. It filled her with peace and reminded her of happier times – it reminded her of Christmas. When she got to know Nick a little better, she'd speak to him about decorating.

The bubbling grease in the fryer caught her attention. If those fries stayed in the fryer much longer they would be ruined. She pulled out the basket, hung it on the basket-hook to drain the grease, and then plopped the fries into a paper-lined basket.

Nick rushed in, eyes wide. "The fries."

"Just took them out." She handed him the basket and a bottle of ketchup.

Nick's brows crinkled. "Thanks."

Chapter Two

Nick uncapped two bottles of beer and handed one to Macy. From a financial standpoint, it had been a great night. He had so many customers that he almost ran out of beer and the cash register was so full it couldn't hold one more dollar; good problems to have. From a physical standpoint, he was beyond exhaustion. If Macy hadn't stepped up, he probably would've crashed an hour ago. She kept the tables clean, made burgers and fries without any guidance, and served a few draughts.

Macy wrinkled her nose. "Not a fan of beer. It tastes like foamy yeast."

For the first time in twelve hours, he wanted to laugh, but he didn't. "Foamy yeast?" He took a big swig to show he disagreed.

She pretended to gag. "I'm more a coffee drinker. Do you mind if I make a pot?"

"Not at all. Help yourself." Nick watched Macy hurry to the coffee maker. This arrangement just might work. While she resembled Francine, she was nothing like the self-centered viper who stepped on his heart with four inch heels. His gaze traveled to Macy's sneakers – sensible shoes that couldn't inflict too much damage. Although, it didn't matter what kind of shoes she wore since a working relationship was the only thing he wanted with Macy Kincade. She could wear ten-inch heels and it wouldn't be a problem, except maybe for her.

Macy indulged in a sip of coffee. "Ahhh."

Nick sat his beer bottle down. "Ready to go over a few things?"

"Just a sec." She pulled a small spiral bound notebook from her purse. "Okay, shoot."

Nick liked her efficiency. "First and foremost, we need to mop up spills right away. And we need to keep up with the puddles from the snow being tracked in." Expecting to get a duh-look like he would've gotten from Francine, he was surprised when Macy wholeheartedly agreed.

"The beer cooler behind the bar needs stocked when it gets low." Again, Nick was amazed that she wrote that down, especially since she'd stocked the cooler earlier without being told.

"Be sure to check I.D.'s for the younger crowd. I don't want to lose my license by selling alcohol to underage kids."

"I had someone bite my head off earlier when I asked for his I.D." Macy's slight frame shook with laughter. "He said, 'listen pipsqueak, I'm older than you'. He shared a few choice words when I still made him produce it."

Nick hated when customers got up in his grill for checking I.D.'s. "Don't let anyone bully you."

"I'm Midge Pennington's granddaughter. Need I say more?"

"Nope." He pictured Macy giving the guy a karate chop to the neck, and had to take a sip of beer to squelch the laugh forming in his belly.

He messed with the label on his bottle. There was one

more important thing he wanted to say, but couldn't get it out. Probably a good thing. If he told her not to get overly friendly with the male customers, she might take it wrong. Truthfully, how she handled the hounds was her business. If she got whisked away to the French Alps, it was of no consequence to him.

Macy asked a few food related questions, but mostly she took notes.

"I wanted to give you a crash course in making mixed drinks and also teach you how to run the cash register, but I'm wiped out. Any chance you could come in a couple hours early tomorrow?"

"Happy to come in whenever you say." Excitement sparkled in her blue eyes. "Any chance you could walk me home tonight?" She lifted her wrist to check the time. "I mean, this morning."

"Walk you home?" It took a second to register that they were now neighbors. He started to frown deeper, but stopped.

* * *

The easy snow that fell earlier was now coming down like confetti, making the walk to the apartment complex an icy adventure. Every step without falling was a feat. If it hadn't been for Nick's strong arms, Macy would've fallen several times. When he steadied her the last time she fell into his chest, bringing their mouths inches from each other. There was a suspended moment where they blinked then stared.

Nick's feet slipped, Macy dugs her heels in, and they remained upright. He took a slight step away.

Macy felt an odd prick of disappointment, which was silly because he didn't want to fall and crack his head anymore than she did. But that tiny inner voice that spoke the truth more times than she cared to hear, chimed in that Nick didn't want her hanging on him – because of the ice, or for any other reason. "We probably should've taken a cab," she said for lack of something better to say.

"It's just a few blocks." Nick was still close enough to grab her if she fell, but far enough away to make her sigh.

Macy wondered what was going through his head. She was certain he struggled with the reality that he had her in his work space, and now in his personal space. Lord knows *she* was struggling, not in the same way. Somehow in the small amount of time from when she walked into Barstow's Tavern until now, something strange…and unwanted…took a hold of her; something pleasurable but ridiculous – attraction. Admitting that made her uncomfortable. She was so not ready to cross that bridge again. Her heart was still a mess from the ratfink. She didn't need to complicate things even more with dreamy thoughts of Nick Barstow. The scent of musk on his skin and a hint of peppermint on his breath were not helping. They toyed with her equilibrium; factor in the icy pavement, and it was a wonder she could walk.

To mask a sudden burst of nervousness, Macy began to ramble. "I'm surprised by all the snow. I didn't think it was supposed to come until Friday. I guess I shouldn't be surprised; after all, it is December. By the way, I noticed you haven't decorated for the holidays."

Nick pulled the collar of his coat up around his neck. "I don't do decorations."

"Why don't you do decorations?" She didn't wait for an answer. "I could take care of the decorating for you."

His response was straight and to the point. "I don't want any Christmas decorations in my bar."

Macy should've let it go at that; she didn't. "You have to put up decorations. It's an unwritten rule – no decorations, no Christmas."

"For the last time, I don't do decorations and I don't do Christmas."

The way Nick enunciated every word made her stop. "Because of your religion?"

Nick's bushy brows gathered so tight they formed a V. "No, not for religious reasons. I'm Catholic. I just don't want any damned decorations or any part of Christmas, okay?"

Macy couldn't fathom anyone ditching the experience of Christmas. She mumbled, "Scrooge," under her breath.

Nick mumbled something that sounded like "Don't push it if you know what's good for you."

Luckily they arrived at the apartment complex without the need for further mumbling.

After they stomped their feet to remove the snow from their shoes, they climbed three sets of stairs instead of taking the elevator.

Macy unlocked the door to her grandmother's apartment. "Thanks so much for hiring me, Nick. And for walking me home." Before she ducked inside, she snorted a laugh. "One small strand of twinkle lights wouldn't hurt."

* * *

Nick tossed his coat into the chair by his bed, bypassed his nightly ritual of brushing his teeth and flossing, stripped down to his boxers and fell into bed. He huffed the accumulated fatigue of the last twelve hours into his pillow. He rolled to his side and expelled another lengthy yawn. He was so tired that he probably wouldn't wake up until it was time to go to work again.

Wrong!

A minute or two later, his eyes popped open. He cursed, hit his pillow, and closed them again. His subconscious, however, had other plans. Nick used his forefingers to hold his eyelids shut. "Go. To. Sleep."

It didn't happen.

Nick dragged his legs to the side of the bed and sat up. Teeth. That was it. He was a creature of habit. Until he brushed his teeth there would be no sleep.

While brushing, thoughts of Macy occupied his brain. "Twinkle lights. Pffft. Not happening," Nick garbled through a mouthful of toothpaste.

He wandered to the refrigerator, opened a bottle of water, and took a huge swig. He caught his reflection in the window above the sink and heaved a heavy sigh. His day began with a scowl, and ended with one. But that's where he needed be. All he wanted to do was scowl his way through December and then move on to the New Year. Sure, it was a stupid, self-indulgent way to deal with the memory of being dumped at Christmastime, but it worked for him, sort of. Now that Macy was in the picture, he wasn't sure what would happen. He had a feeling she would dig until she got to the heart of the scowl and she'd try to change his outlook on Christmas. She'd turn into Midge and try to fix him. Realistically, the only one who could fix things was Francine. He'd given the witch his heart, and she still owned it.

Chapter Three

Nick was tempted to drink Macy's mistakes, but he didn't go for mix drinks. Give him a beer any day. "There's no whiskey in a Long-Island iced tea." He dumped the concoction down the drain.

Macy apologized all over the place. "Sorry to waste your liquor. I thought I had it down pat." She puffed out her cheeks. "I've looked at the drink guide so many times my eyes are starting to cross. Arghhhh. It shouldn't be that difficult to make mix drinks."

"Don't stress yourself out. You'll get it." Nick wandered to the far end of the bar to get away from the sweet smell of her perfume. It was overwhelming, not in the sense that she wore too much. Every time she moved he caught a whiff of something lightly floral. He liked it, and didn't like that he did.

Nick looked at the clock on the back wall. "If tonight is a carbon copy of last night, we'll want to eat a bite now. We may not get a chance later. Are you up for some chicken strips and a chef salad?"

"Sounds like a plan. I'll make the salads." Her blue eyes glistened the way Midge's did when she was about zing him with a comment. "I bet you like honey mustard dressing."

"Oh yeah? Why is that?"

"Sweet with a hint of sour."

Him? Or the dressing? Nick narrowed his eyes. He did not want this kind of interaction. It felt like flirting, and he did not want to flirt. "I like ranch." Blatant fib. He loved honey mustard.

Nick threw a bar towel over his shoulder and pushed through the double doors to the kitchen. Macy was on his heels.

"My grandmother said…"

Here we go.

Macy smiled softly like it would keep the wall down that would go up if he didn't like what he heard. Nick cordoned himself off with an additional barricade – the freezer door.

Macy waited until he stepped back out with a bag of chicken strips before she tried to scale the wall. "She said you're having a hard time dealing with your breakup from Francine. Would you like to talk about it?"

Nick dropped a handful of chicken strips into the fryer at the same time she asked the question. A splat of grease caught him off guard and burned his hand. He cursed and Macy took a step back. "No," he sneered. "I do not want to talk about it." *Midgeeeeee!* When he got a hold of her he would wring her neck. She was trying to mess with his life through her granddaughter. She needed to stop. He was happy with his life. Kind of. Hell, not at all. But that was his problem, not hers.

He moved to the dishwasher in another attempt to put distance between he and Macy. Again, she moved with him. The infuriating woman was determined to share more than her perfume. Nick removed a stack of still-warm ten-inch dinner plates from the dishwasher and sat them on the counter with a clunk. Macy flinched.

"Sometimes talking about it can help. Lord knows I could've used someone to talk to when things fell apart with me and the ratfink."

Nick remembered Midge bending his ear awhile back about Macy. Something about her parents moving to Arizona for health reasons, leaving Macy on her own. Still, she had Midge. But talking to your grandma about affairs of the heart wasn't something he'd want to do either. Regardless, he and Macy weren't going to have a conversation about Francine. "I hired you to be a barmaid, not my therapist." He put his hands on his hips.

Macy didn't appear affected by his sudden loud tone. She twisted her lips to the side and studied him. "I'm just saying…"

Nick put his palm up. "You listen like your grandmother does." He returned to the fryer and removed the chicken strips. He dropped them in a paper-lined basket and motioned for her to follow. He took a seat at the bar. Macy sat a salad in front of him and then perched on the adjacent stool.

She took a nibble of lettuce and laid her fork aside.

He braced for more.

Macy swiveled toward him. "What makes a guy suddenly decide he doesn't want to be married?"

Nick practically choked on his bite of chicken. He wiped his mouth with a napkin. He was tempted to ask the same question, just worded differently – why does a woman suddenly decide she doesn't want to get married? "I'm not sure I can give you the answer you want, Macy." He tried to lighten the conversation. "I've heard women say you can put us men in a bag, shake it up, and when you dump us out it's hard to tell one from the other." He shrugged. "Seriously, we're not all alike. We're driven by different demons, just like women."

Macy surprised him with an eye-roll. "Nice dodge, Barstow."

He wanted to laugh, but he wasn't ready to give her that much leverage over his mood. Nick stole her line, "Just saying."

* * *

Macy wanted Nick to let her in, but he kept the deadbolt of his life securely in place. He made it clear it would stay that way. If she was smart she'd leave him the heck alone. She shuffled to the end of the bar to Jim Simmons. Jim introduced himself last night and had his radar locked on her ever since. "Ready for another beer?"

Jim beamed a grin, shoved his mug across the bar, and tossed a five dollar bill into the tip jar. "Yep. And I could go for a burger with all the trimmings…on one condition."

She didn't want to ask. "What condition?"

Jim patted the empty stool next to him. "That you have one with me."

"A beer or a burger?"

"Both." He added "sweetheart" and Macy cringed.

Last night Macy put Jim into the not-going-to-happen-in-this-lifetime category. While he was attractive, she wasn't attracted to him. Not even a little. "I don't drink beer. And I'm not hungry. Thanks for the offer."

"Barstow," Jim hollered to get Nick's attention. "Tell Macy she has to have a drink with me."

Nick's constant frown deepened. "She's working." A muscle ticked in his jaw.

Jim blew off Nick's surly reply to focus on Macy. "At least

have a cup of coffee with me. Nick and I are buddies; he won't care if you take a break."

Macy was thankful happy hour was underway. A group of guys crowded into the tavern, followed by two women dressed in business suits. The guys took the last table in the center of the room so they could watch sports on the flat screen TV; leaving the women to take the last two bar stools, which included the empty one next to Jim. Macy pretended to be disappointed. "What can I get you gals?"

"White wine spritzers," they said in unison.

Nick walked by. "White wine and club soda," he said quietly as if he didn't want to embarrass her for not knowing.

After Macy made the drinks she headed to the table of guys who were divided in their allegiance to footballs teams. Half of the group howled with happiness when the sportscaster replayed the winning touchdown – from every angle – of the football game the night before. The other half of the group booed.

"What can I get you boys?" The innocent question received a raunchy response. Macy blushed all the way to her toes.

Nick obviously heard. "Keep it clean or leave," he warned.

One guy piped up that Nick didn't need to be Macy's guard dog. Another one told him not to get his boxers in a bunch.

"I'm serious," Nick said from behind the bar. "If you don't behave, you can find another bar."

The ringleader apologized.

Macy took their drink order and hurried to Nick. "I need Sex on the Beach."

Of course she meant the drink, but it didn't stop Nick's

thoughts from going haywire. Normally, his fantasies veered to Francine. Not this time. He looked away from Macy so she couldn't read his thoughts. "Vodka, peach schnapps, cranberry juice, and orange juice." He shoved the drink guide in her direction and hurried off with a tray filled with drinks.

His customers were satisfied for the moment and his gaze navigated around the room until it settled on Macy. The soft sashay of her hips reeled him in. He started to smile and instantly caught his reaction. He needed a distraction.

Nick grabbed the shovel and bag of salt that was stowed by the door. "I'll be outside for a little bit."

The air had a bite but it was peaceful. Lampposts illuminated the falling snowflakes and an occasional gust of wind sent them swirling. This is where he needed to be; not inside with the temptation of Macy. It bothered him that he was noticing things about her that he shouldn't – the way her blue eyes sparkled when she spoke, the sweet pink of her lips, her friendly interaction with customers, how she went at a task until it was complete. There were so many things about this woman that he liked. Those same things were a mental hassle.

The scrape of the shovel against the pavement sidetracked his thoughts. After he removed as much snow as possible, he scattered salt to melt the rest.

A few patrons stepped out of the tavern to smoke. One of the guys leaned against the building, took a few puffs, and hit Nick with a question that his ears wanted to reject. "Is Macy available?"

Macy was not his territory but Nick felt the need to protect her anyway. "She's not available."

Another guy snorted a laugh between puffs. "I didn't see a ring on her finger, so she's fair game."

"Who's fair game?"

Nick recognized the voice. "Hello, Midge." His spritely neighbor was bundled up so tight you could only see a portion of her face. He wrapped her in a hug.

"Hello, stud." She leaned up to peck his cheek with a kiss. "Now, who's fair game?"

Nick had an inkling she knew who the guy referred to. He lifted both brows and let the puffing hound bury himself.

"Macy," the guy said. "I wouldn't mind taking that little delicacy home tonight."

Nick was close enough to see the dynamite spark in Midge's eyes.

Midge pulled out of his embrace to poke the hound in the chest. "That's my granddaughter you're talking about and no one is taking her home tonight," she grinned like a conspiring ole granny, "except for Nick." She poked the guy harder. "He and Macy are involved and I don't want you messing it up."

The guy set hard eyes on Midge. Nick latched onto her arm. "Time to go inside, Midge."

Midge mumbled under her breath that if the guy said one more word about Macy he was getting a karate chop to the neck. Surprisingly, she went inside before Nick had to lift her to the guys' neck.

"Why didn't you say you and Macy had a thing, Barstow?"

Because we don't. And they never would. He was still in love with Francine.

"Gram! What are you doing here?" Macy was excited to see her grandmother.

"I couldn't live without one of Nick's famous chef salads," Midge spouted.

Macy lifted a brow of suspicion. "You don't like salad."

Midge offered a sheepish grin and slid onto a bar stool. "Maybe I wanted to see how things were going."

"Uh-huh. I see." Macy teased with clear accusation.

"Okay, I'm downright nosey. There. I said it." Midge laughed like telling the truth was something funny.

Macy wandered to the other side of the bar to embrace the woman who made life a little crazy but interesting. "I love ya, Gram. Now, what can I get you?"

"Scotch and chicken strips."

Macy pointed both forefingers at her grandmother. "Weird combination, but you're the boss. Be back in a couple of minutes." She took off toward the kitchen.

Midge said something that made Macy stop in her tracks. "I told a little white lie when I was outside."

"How little?" Macy had a feeling it was a whopper. Her grandmother thrived on keeping the pot stirred. Since she was confessing right away, whatever she'd said couldn't be good.

Midge shrugged.

Macy traced the few steps back to her grandmother. "You didn't get me in trouble with Nick, did you?"

The old gal shook her head. "Of course not. Just the opposite. You can thank me by giving me the scotch and chicken strips for free."

Someone from a corner table hollered to get her attention. "Gotta go. When I get back be prepared to spill your guts." Nick hadn't come back inside so there was a better than good chance he wasn't happy with whatever her grandmother had said; although, he never appeared happy so it would be hard to tell.

Chapter Four

Nick dilly-dallied outside longer than he should have. When he finally went back inside Macy was up to her elbows in orders.

"About time you returned, Barstow," she said without any suggestion of annoyance.

Anyone else would've read him the riot act. He deserved the riot act. "I know" was all he offered. He grabbed one of the bigger trays from behind the bar and bussed a couple of tables to make room for a fresh batch of customers.

He kept an eye peeled for the hound from outside. To the hounds' benefit he didn't return to the bar.

Nick looked for Midge and found her knee-deep in conversation with Jim Simmons. Good. She couldn't get in too much trouble with Jim. At least he hoped not.

It took a handful of hours for the crowd to thin. If he could get a few more people to leave he could relax. He was overtired and in need of a stiff cup of coffee, or a half dozen bottles of beer. Nick searched for Macy. She had to be dog-tired too. From the time he flipped over the closed sign to open, the place was full. Either the approaching holidays accounted for the extra business, or his new barmaid was the big draw. Maybe a little of both? Macy did have an upbeat personality and was fine to look at, obviously word had gotten out.

Nick spied her behind the bar making a fresh pot of coffee.

Midge slithered next to him. "Well, sweetheart, it's time for me to head home."

Nick wrapped her in a hug. "If you could hang around for another half hour, Macy and I could walk you home."

Midge waved off the proposal. "Don't worry yourself. Jim has already called a taxi for us." She lowered her voice. "He's had one too many beers." She nodded toward Macy and then gave Nick a wink. "You two lovebirds have a good time."

Nick started to balk.

"Uh. Uh." Midge put a finger to his lips. "Don't discount the idea." She laid a hand across his heart. "This bad boy needs Macy."

Jim came to claim Midge, not a minute too soon. "Time to take this amazing woman home." He whispered to Nick. "She's had a little too much scotch."

Two of a kind. Both had a fondness for hooch and for making him nuts. Midge's lovebird comment made him shake his head. Older people fell into two categories: wise and pains in the neck. Midge fell into both; right now she was hogging the second category. But the things she said – wacky, or not – made him think.

Nick joined Macy at the coffee pot. "I so need a cup of coffee."

"You might have to make your own. I have dibs on this pot." She yawned then followed up with a chuckle. "Don't frown." She touched his forehead. "I was kidding. I'll share."

Nick did not want Macy touching him. He couldn't think straight when she did.

* * *

It was twenty minutes past closing time and the last two people were still downing brew like it was nectar of the gods. Macy and Nick killed a pot of coffee while they waited for them to leave. She was thankful when Nick finally piped up that it was time for them to go. He received a "boo". The couple vacated their chairs and headed for the door. They wobbled when they walked.

"Can I call you a cab?" Macy asked.

"Nah. We just moved in two doors down."

Two doors down was a bookstore. "Above the bookstore, I assume?"

"Yep," the woman slurred. "It's real cozy."

Nick wove the woman's arm through his, and did the same to her husband. "It's icy out there."

Macy watched Nick guide them out. Five minutes later, he was back, shivering and brushing snow off of his shirt. "I should have taken the time to put on a coat."

She held up a cup of freshly brewed coffee from the new pot she made in his absence. "This should help."

"Awesome. Let's take it to the stock room. We need to put some things away before we leave."

Stock room? Tight quarters. A chance of brushing against Nick. Not a good idea. But she wasn't a wuss.

It took fifteen minutes to stash half of the delivery.

Macy yawned.

Nick yawned.

"We need more java." He grabbed her cup and headed to the bar.

With him temporarily gone, Macy tried to clear her head. As predicted, they bumped into each other a couple of times and a blasted heat wave crashed across her. She was tempted to make a trip to the walk-in cooler to cool off but she had no good excuse; well, she had one, but in no way would it be shared.

Nick returned. Instead of juggling two cups of hot coffee, he had the empty cups on one thumb and carried the entire pot in his free hand. "I'm so worn out I won't have to worry about caffeine keeping me awake."

"Same here." She might not be able to sleep but caffeine wouldn't be the culprit.

Macy pulled an empty crate from the corner for the coffee pot.

Nick poured them each a cup. He sat his cup down and looked around the tiny room. "This stuff can wait until tomorrow. Let's enjoy our coffee." He retrieved two more empty crates and sat them across from each other. "Have a seat."

"Gladly."

Their knees touched. Macy moved hers to the right. Nick moved his to the left.

Macy took a sip of coffee and made a soft sound of appreciation. Nick's gaze connected with hers, and she could feel a blush creep up her neck. Soon it would be in her cheeks.

A few awkward seconds ticked by.

"My ex called today." Ack! Where did that come from? Macy had been trying to forget the irritating phone call but her subconscious must've grown tired of storing it all day. And now it was out.

Nick tried to look uninterested but they were so close she didn't miss the fleeting glimmer in his brown eyes. Macy wasn't sure she should burden him with her troubles.

"Oh yeah?" Nick shifted on the crate. It was late. He was tired. And he didn't want to get personal. Well, he wanted to, not in the way Macy did. His eyes dropped to her mouth. He'd been homing in on those luscious lips since she started working for him. Today, the pull was extra strong.

Macy sighed. "The ratfink chewed me out for selling the house too cheap." She rubbed her forehead. "I ran the amount past him before I accepted the customer's offer. Apparently one of his buddies made a huge deal out of it last night and the rat took it out on me this morning."

Nick felt her pain. Ex's were too much to deal with sometimes. But he didn't have any comforting words to offer. Instead, he leaned forward and brushed her lips with a brief kiss. Why he did something so personal and impulsive was beyond comprehension. Lethargy obviously blocked brain waves.

He drew back.

She drew back.

"Macy, I..." He had nothing. "Shouldn't have done that. Exhaustion is kicking my butt tonight. We should go." He didn't wait for her reaction. *Stupid. Stupid. Stupid.* Nick wanted to hit his forehead with his palm. But he didn't want to let on that the kiss bothered him. Although, he was pretty sure she knew.

Nick stayed a few steps ahead of Macy. It was the only way to deal with the shock of something so...pleasant.

He reached the coat hooks, removed both their coats, and handed Macy hers without looking her in the eye. "I need to shovel the sidewalk again and scatter some salt."

Macy handed Nick the shovel. She grabbed the bag of salt.

In silence they cleared the snow. When the shovel and bag of salt were tucked away, they walked home in an even deeper silence.

Nick laced his fingers through Macy's. He didn't want her to fall.

Chapter Five

Expecting Macy to answer the door, Nick was surprised to be greeted by Midge. She looked a little haggard around the edges. No doubt the result of too much scotch and staying up so late. "Hey, good looking." He tweaked Midge's chin like he always did. "Is your granddaughter rested up?"

"Yep." Midge latched onto his arm and tugged him inside. "It's a pie kind of day. Join me."

The smell of coconut cream pie filled the kitchen and Nick's mouth watered. But he didn't have time for pie. "Is Macy almost ready?"

"She's been ready for a few hours." Midge took two small plates from the cabinet and pointed to a kitchen chair. "You're always in a rush, Nick. Humor an old lady, have pie with me."

When Midge got something in her head, it was wise to comply. He sat.

Midge cut two hefty slices. She handed one to Nick and propped herself against the kitchen counter with hers. "Would you like coffee to go with that?"

"That would be great."

She sat two steaming cups of coffee on the table, slid into the chair across from him, and eyed him over the rim of her cup. "Today is the feast of St. Nicholas."

Nick lifted an eyebrow. "Is that right?" Where was Macy? He didn't hear her fumbling around.

"St. Nicholas had a reputation for secret gift-giving."

Okay. That was a weird comment. "Apparently not so secret."

"Nick Barstow, are you mocking me?"

"Never. I'm just wondering what this is leading to." He took a huge bite of pie. "Good stuff." He licked his lips.

"Glad you like it." Midge went to take a bite, but laid the forkful of pie back on her plate. "Could I ask for a secret-gift?"

He had a feeling she was setting him up for something and he was certain it involved Macy, especially after the love-bird comment from last night. "What would you like?"

Mischief beamed from those aged eyes. "For you to give Macy a break."

An even weirder comment. Nick studied Midge. It was clear she was trying to hook them up. He messed with the meringue on top of his pie. "I did. I hired her."

"I know. And I'm forever grateful. But she needs more."

"Explain *more*."

"Well," she tapped the side of her coffee cup, "how do I put this?"

"Just ask, Midge. I have to get going."

The mischief was gone. Midge patted his arm. "Macy isn't here right now because she's out delivering resumes."

A measure of disappointment filled his chest. Even if he didn't want to hook up with Macy, he enjoyed their walks to and from work. It finally sank in that she was job hunting. "Delivering resumes?"

"She's looking for a different job, Nick."

The information bothered the hell out of him. "I'm obviously missing something here so you're going to have to catch me up with what you want me to do. What secret gift can I give you? And what does it have to do with Macy looking for another job?"

"Since you're in an all-fired hurry, here's the high-points. A girl can't survive in New York without a healthy wage, so give her a raise. And so her talent doesn't go to waste, make her your bookkeeper."

"I can raise her pay. But I like to keep my own books, thank you very much."

"She's gonna leave, Nick."

"Why is this so important to you, Midge? I mean, Macy deserves to work in a place that will give her health insurance. Maybe even some dental coverage."

"Do I have to karate chop your neck to make you understand?"

"I guess so."

Midge leaned forward to gently touch his cheek. "If Macy hangs around long enough, maybe you'll fall for her. She'll be happy. You'll be happy. And I can stop worrying about the two of you."

* * *

Nick paced behind the bar. He'd cleared the snow. Finished unpacking and putting things away in the stock room. Changed the grease in the fryer. Made a pot of coffee. And was going nuts waiting for Macy.

He didn't want her to quit. It was selfish on his part but the thought of her leaving upset him. Was it really wages causing her to move on? Or was it because of the kiss? It had bothered him. Maybe it bothered her too. Or was it because she tried to vent about her ex and he stopped her with a kiss?

He scoffed at Midge's distorted way of thinking – keep Macy on so they would fall for each other. Wasn't going to happen. That kiss was impulsive. There wasn't anything behind it. When two overly-tired people were cooped up together things were bound to happen.

Nick checked his watch. She was ten minutes late. He sighed. Maybe she already had a new job and wouldn't come in tonight.

The bells above the door chimed and Nick's heart leapt from his chest.

A group of three women, none of them Macy, entered the tavern. "Sir," one of the women spoke up. "We're collecting money for needy children this Christmas. Would you care to make a donation?"

St. Nicholas popped into his thoughts, thanks to Midge.

Before he could answer, Macy stepped from behind the women. "Sorry I'm late, Nick." She shrugged out of her coat.

Nick focused on Macy. There was an extra spring to her step. Sure enough, she would be leaving him. As soon as these ladies were gone, she'd share the news.

"Ahem. Sir. We're collecting for needy children."

"Just a sec." Nick hurried to the small drawer below the cash register where he kept his wallet. He pulled out a wad of bills and shoved them in the woman's hand.

The lady's eyes grew big. "Thank you, sir."

"You're welcome."

He waited until they left before he grilled Macy. "Midge says you're leaving."

Macy sat on a bar stool and swiveled toward him. "I'm not. At least not for awhile. No one is hiring until after the first of the year."

It was wrong to be happy that she struck out.

* * *

Macy was torn. What she failed to tell Nick was that she received two job offers this afternoon. Both companies wanted her, but not until the New Year. So she didn't exactly lie to him, just conveniently left out a few details. He might not care that she left, but the thought of not seeing him every day messed with her head.

Last night she laid awake thinking about the kiss and how Nick reacted afterward. He appeared uncomfortable that it happened. Macy hoped he didn't regret it. God, she hoped he didn't. For her, it was a game changer. She planned earlier in the week to go job hunting this morning. When she woke up, she had to coax herself to go through with it. Now that she had two offers on the table, she didn't know what the heck to do.

"Giving money to that organization was a really sweet thing to do. It was for Christmas, Nick." Maybe there was hope for him yet. Maybe he had a hidden Christmas spirit dying to get out.

"Don't get too excited. I'm still a jerk." He started to walk toward the kitchen.

"No you're not." Macy tugged the back of his shirt to stop him. It was a bold move that made him swing around. She squared her shoulders like it would lend credence to her words. "My grandmother isn't fond of jerks; therefore, you're not." When Nick started to speak she shushed him. "Don't diss my gram."

A group of men in business suits saved Macy from getting an earful.

Chapter Six

It was hard to believe it was December twenty-third already. Where had the time gone? He should be happy that the month was almost over, but Nick was in a foul mood. A lethal frame of mind was more like it. He'd be wise to stay home from the tavern. Since he was the owner, it wouldn't happen. He had to get dressed, put one foot in front of the other and deal with the third anniversary of no-anniversary. Exactly three years ago, Francine Vanguard pulled the rug out from under him. And for exactly three years he'd been stuck in a giant sinkhole.

Nick made a low growling noise. People kept throwing him a ladder and he kept tossing it back. He thought about Macy. She'd been trying to pull him out barehanded. He'd take her hand, then let go. She hadn't given up on him. For the last three weeks she was sweet and made opportunities to reassure him that he wasn't a jerk. There were no more kissing encounters in the storage room, although a few nights he'd entertained the idea. Thank goodness he came to his senses before he made it happen.

Tonight, he was in no mood to be told he wasn't a jerk. He didn't want Macy being sweet. He wanted to be left alone.

* * *

Nick had been crabbing since they opened, and Macy had been doing her best to stay out of his way. Although the way he was biting heads off, she'd be missing hers very soon. She'd gotten a big hint that he was in an even bigger funk than usual during the walk from the apartment building to the tavern. He growled at the sun for ducking in and out of the clouds. She almost gave him a playful shove, but he looked dead serious. When they got to work, the beer distributors' head was first on the chopping block. The guy arrived fifteen minutes later than normal, Nick came unglued. The driver explained he was caught in stopped traffic. Nick ranted that he should always be prepared for the unexpected. Seriously? Prepare for stopped traffic?

Second victim, the produce guy who forgot the lettuce. The dishwasher received a verbal bashing for taking too long. There was a sticky spot in the floor that Macy must've missed when she mopped last night that ticked him off. *Sheesh.* Nick needed to take a chill pill or get a distemper shot, Macy wouldn't mention it. She decided to let whatever was ailing him play out.

For the next hour, he frowned, glared, grumbled under his breath, and then as if he couldn't hold back any longer with Macy, she became another casualty of his mood.

"Get the lead out, Macy. Table four needs silverware and napkins."

This bad mood thing was getting a little old and it was starting to rub off. Macy was close to telling him to shove it. Instead, she took a breath, kept her expression even and went into a silent spiel that table four was Nick's, not hers. After delivering the silverware and napkins, she joined Nick behind the bar to have a word with him about his disposition.

Nick didn't give her a chance. He turned away from the prying eyes and ears of his customers and bit into Macy. "You were supposed to remind me to order maraschino cherries and club soda."

"You didn't tell me anything of the sort. Note to self: buy Nick a notepad so he can write things down, or learn how to read his mind." She might as well have thrown a handful of firecrackers into a roaring fire.

If a look could tear a person apart, those slicer-dicer brown eyes just removed her right ear and shoulder. "You're the reason I work alone." His words hissed between pearly-white, clenched teeth.

Macy wouldn't point out that he *didn't* work alone. "You're the reason God made chocolate." It was a silly comment meant to lighten things up. Nick, however, was so deep in the muck of his mood that he didn't as much as blink.

Jim Simmons had left for awhile, but came back and took his usual seat at the end of the bar. He hollered for a cold one. Macy and Nick engaged in a stare-down. Jim reiterated his request. "Earth to Macy."

Nick's eyes hardened a little more around the edges. "Your *friend* needs a beer."

Her friend? Macy purposely hardened her eyes to match his. "Watch it, Barstow." She pulled a frosty mug from the freezer, filled it with Jim's favorite draught beer, and glared at Nick as she brushed past him to deliver the beer. Was Nick jealous that she got Jim's attention instead of him?

Macy shivered at Jim's lascivious grin. Euw! She'd already

drawn the conclusion that Jim was semi-attractive but not her type, but he wasn't getting the message. Every day he worked hard to get her to notice him. It wasn't going to happen. The guy drank too much. Had no outside interests. And spit when he talked. She managed to sidestep his advances…and his spit…so far.

"Hey, good lookin'." Jim reached for the beer before she was even ten feet away.

"How's it going, Jim?" She kept her voice free of enthusiasm. No use sending mixed messages.

"It's going great, sweetheart." He grinned and pointed to something beside him.

Macy was afraid to look. She peered over the edge of the bar. "What is it?"

Jim winked. "Something for you."

Macy shook her head, not comfortable with this odd turn of events. "I can't accept gifts."

He laughed like it was no big deal. "Boss's orders?"

"No. Mine," she stated flatly.

Jim guzzled half his beer. "For someone who looks so fine, you're a stick in the mud." He laughed.

Macy had the good sense to laugh too. "Yep." She wandered off, disregarding Jim and whatever was in the black, plastic sack beside him. She was happy that the rambunctious happy-hour crowd arrived.

The next two hours were a whirlwind of beer, sandwiches, and salads. She was happy for the chaos, but wondered if it was enough commotion to thaw Nick's frosty behavior.

It wasn't.

She had to chip ice off of him to find out how to make a B-52 since it wasn't on the laminated drink guide. He rattled off the ingredients but he acted like it was a pain to share the information.

Nick Barstow was a hair away from being put in a sleeper hold.

Macy slanted a look at the clock. With all the extra business that came with the holidays, they'd been pulling twelve-hour shifts. Eight hours to go. She expelled a noiseless sigh. If Nick stayed sour, this could very well be the last shift she put in at Barstow's Tavern. Good thing she had something to fall back on. Maybe that was his grand plan all along – tick her off so she would quit, so he could resume working alone. The last few days he'd been a bear, and she was able to keep him from mangling customers by taking the brunt of his mood. Tonight, he was more of a crocodile, ready to sink his sharp teeth into anyone who looked at him wrong.

* * *

Nick found Macy in the kitchen staring out the window with her arms wrapped around her. He wanted to apologize for being a jackass, but there was no time, he had five food orders to fill. He dropped a basket of fries into the fryer. The familiar sizzle when the frozen fries met the hot oil didn't happen. He checked the pilot light and found it out. Arghhh! The last time the darned thing was out he had to replace the hi-limit. He did not have time for this kind of nonsense.

Macy must've heard his groan even though he'd kept it internal. "What's wrong?"

"Everything." He slapped burgers on the grill so hard his thumb made contact with the heat. He brushed off the pain and hurried to the cooler for five chef salads, which would be on the house since he couldn't produce the fries.

"What can I do?"

The concern in her voice got to him, but he wasn't ready to be soothed. "Nothing." He plopped the salads on a tray, dumped a handful of dressing packets on too, and shoved through the double doors.

The customers expecting fries looked at each other when he sat salads in front of them. "The fryer is being a pain so there won't be any fries. The only thing you have to pay for is your drinks." Expecting some serious grumbling he was surprised when the ladies engaged in high-fives.

On his way back to the kitchen, something shimmery caught his eye. He stopped in his tracks to zero in on the object reflecting in the mirror behind the bar. Was that a…? He trekked over to verify that stashed on the shelf just below the whiskey display was indeed a miniature battery-operated Christmas tree. A series of curse words fired through his brain.

Macy flinched when he barreled into kitchen.

Whatever she had in her hand hit the floor. Nick pinned her with authority. "What part of no-Christmas-decorations don't you understand?"

A hurt look crumbled Macy's expression. Her bottom lip quivered ever so slightly. To his surprise, she squared her shoulders, untied her apron, and threw it against his chest. "I seriously have no idea what you're talking about. Frankly, I don't care. For the last few weeks you've made it plain that you're happier working alone. Well, have at it." She walked off without stomping.

Nick watched her go. Part of him wanted to stay exactly where he was. The other part called him a fool and prompted him to set chase.

Before he took a step, the bubbling of the fryer and the smell of French fries caught his attention. He recalled something falling to the floor when he walked in. His gaze dropped to the lighter that was now halfway under the stainless steel counter. Something as simple as a lighter shook him to the core. He'd been worse than a jerk to Macy – and to everyone else – yet she took the time to mess with the fryer. As insignificant as that would seem to someone else, it meant more than just a working fryer – it meant she cared.

His feet moved before his brain could catch up. "Macy!"

Jim kinked the pursuit. "Too late, buddy. She ran out the door before I could show her the Christmas tree I brought."

"That's your tree?" The air seized in Nick's lungs. He slumped against the door jamb, regret poking him from the inside out.

"Yeah. Pretty cool, huh?"

"You're a blockhead, Simmons. Because of you, she's gone."

Jim drew back. "Because of me? What have you been smoking?" He shook his head. "Hate to tell ya, Nick, Macy's gone because you don't know how to treat people who care about you." He lifted an eyebrow. "I put up with your bitter disposition because I like the place, and because I know your grumpy mood will pass. Macy has never seen you be anything but grumpy yet her eyes sparkle when she looks at you. I don't get it. I'm nice and she won't pay me a bit of attention."

"Her eyes don't sparkle when…" Nick's words faded while his mind scrambled to accept the possibility.

"They do, Nick." Jim shrugged.

A tumble of emotions rocked him all at once. He liked Macy. More than liked her. The inner voice that normally kept him grounded, rallied forward with a powerful thought – that he loved Macy. He fought the idea…for no more than a second.

The frown that occupied his face since the first of the month started to slide away.

Nick pulled his coat from the hook by the door. He tossed the tavern keys to Jim. "You're in charge." Before he could step outside, the woman who haunted his dreams stepped in.

Every head in the place turned to admire the voluptuous brunette with the come-hither persona.

Nick's eyes widened in shock, but his heart didn't go crazy like he thought it would. It was the damndest thing – there was no sharp intake of excitement, no pulse beating so hard his temples hurt, no feeling of relief that she'd come back. Nothing except annoyance.

Francine's eyes were smudged with mascara like she'd been crying. "Nicky," she said softly.

She always called him Nicky when she tried to schmooze him. "Francine," he replied blankly. It bothered him that he just now realized that.

"I'm so sorry, Nicky." She moved in close, accompanied by the heavy scent of jasmine he thought he could never get enough of. Now he wanted to cough or sneeze to clear his airways.

The hair on the back of his neck prickled like he was about to be struck by lightning. His invisible Kevlar slipped into place. He did not want to deal with Francine. Not now. Not ever. All those feelings he battled since she'd left, fled to higher ground. They didn't want any part of her either. "What brings you to Barstow's?"

Francine's voice splintered. "Aren't you happy to see me?"

About as happy as someone who'd just been stung by a swarm of bees. "Are you daft?" The question was aimed more at himself than her. Why was he wasting time with Francine when he could go after Macy?

Francine's brown eyes blazed with golden flecks of fire. "Is that any way to treat the woman who's been beating herself up for making the biggest mistake of her life?"

Maniacal laughter started in Nick's belly and worked its way up. Oddly, there wasn't an ounce of humor attached to it. "It took you three years to decide you made a mistake?" He couldn't restrain the sarcasm. "I don't see any bruises."

"Huh?" It took a second for his comments to sink in. Her mouth puckered in a pout.

Unaffected, Nick crossed his arms and stood with his feet apart.

Francine sniffed and put a hand on his arm. Nick let his arms drop so hers would too.

"I didn't stop loving you." She pushed against him. "Let me come back to work for you and we'll fix the rough spots in our relationship."

"You didn't stop loving me? Rough spots?" He repeated the questions two more times, each time a little louder. Nick was more flabbergasted than mad. "You walked out the night before our wedding with a guy who took you to the French Alps." He straight-armed her to get her off of him. "There was never any love on your part." His heart and brain finally got it. And he wondered why he wasted so much time brooding over something that never was. Deep down he'd known it, but subconsciously must have clung to the pain as a way to keep from getting hurt again. The scowling bit was added insurance.

"Nicky," she whined.

The shackles that held him to the past, released. A brilliant moment of clarity hit him with enough force to knock him back a step – he was in love with Macy. With every fiber of his being he loved her. It was an incredible revelation that he couldn't wait to share. The scowl and burden he'd been carrying around…gone.

"I wish you the best of luck with your life, Francine; a life that won't include me. And I really wish you'd cart yourself into another time zone."

The bells above the door chimed.

Nick took a sharp intake of excitement, his pulse beat so hard his temples hurt, and a feeling of pure relief enveloped him when he caught sight of a familiar head of blonde hair. Macy was back!

Their gazes connected.

"Macy!" Nick closed the distance between them and swooped her into his arms.

Tears leaked from the corners of her eyes. "I had to come back." She clutched his shoulders like he was life support, and Nick felt the warmth all the way to his soul.

"I'm so sorry. I've been an idiot, Macy."

"Shh." She put a finger to his lips. "Just kiss me."

Nick stood her upright, gathered her in a powerful embrace and kissed her like *she* was life support. Only when they were short of breath did they separate. "I love you, Macy. We've only known each other for a short time, but I've been in love with you…forever. I just had to wise up to realize that you're the one I can't live without."

A round of applause filled the bar.

"I'm in love with you too, Nick. That's why I came back – to convince you that we are meant to be together." Macy planted a series of kisses on his mouth, the tip of his nose and his forehead.

"You've seen me at my worst and still want me. It has to be love." He chuckled tenderly.

Macy put a hand on her heart and one on Nick's. "I can't imagine going a day without you, so I'm staying put. If you don't mind, I'm going to keep working for you to..." she gestured around the bar, "...see where this love takes us."

Nick laid his forehead against Macy's and blocked out the excitement of the crowd that had gathered around. "I'll tell you where this is going to take us, sweetheart...to the altar. I want to marry you, Macy. I don't want to rush you. When you're ready, please marry me."

Macy whispered so only he could hear. "I love you too, Nick Barstow. Would tomorrow be too soon?"

Nick parted them ever so slightly. Love sparkled in Macy's blue eyes and he could feel the high-grade duct tape that had held his heart together, fall away. And he knew without a doubt that this was right. He claimed her mouth in a love-sealing, marriage-proposing, kiss of joy. "You've healed my heart, Macy. And I can't wait until tomorrow."

"You've healed my heart too, Nick." Macy's words were warm, but quickly turned playful. "I forgot to mention one tiny little condition to marrying you."

Nick arched an eyebrow and lifted Macy's hand to kiss her palm. "Anything. Name it."

"You have to let me decorate. Tomorrow is Christmas Eve and I won't set foot in this bar unless it looks like Christmas."

"I love you, Macy. How can I refuse you a simple strand of twinkle lights?"

Completely in charge, Macy alternated kissing Nick and

teasing him. “A strand of twinkle lights? This place is going to be lit up like Rockefeller Center.”

# # #

The Lone White Rose

EVAN

By: Laura Ricker

Prologue

They always say that you don't know what you've got until it's gone. Luckily for Evan Moore, the love of his life wasn't gone yet. She was not officially a married woman until New Year's Eve. That meant he still had time. Time to tell her he made a mistake all those years ago and that he was the one she was supposed to marry. Why had he not realized this earlier? There she was, right in front of his nose, and he took her existence for granted. Now that she had made a promise to marry someone else, it all came rushing back like giant waves beating down on the unsuspecting sand. He loved her with all his heart and wanted nothing more than to hold her in his arms, to tell her what she meant to him. He longed to run his fingers through her long, unbelievably soft, blonde hair and smell her perfume. That is why he was coming back…to pour out his heart and hope she would feel the same way.

After stopping at the flower shop to pick out a bouquet of white roses, Evan made his way back to the church. White roses were her favorite. Whenever he saw a white rose, he thought about her and what they once shared. If couples had flowers like states did, the white rose would definitely be theirs. The snow was falling heavier now than when he first ventured out. It was actually quite beautiful. The fresh flakes blanketed the ground and sparkled in the moonlight like small diamonds scattered on the earth.

Evan made his way through town, going over the things he would say to her. He figured as long as he was honest and spoke from the heart, there was nothing more to do than await her response. A response that could change his life forever; possibly make him the happiest man on the planet. As he approached the final stop light in town, a feeling of excitement came over him. Soon he would know. As the light turned red, the excitement was replaced with a small amount of panic.

The snow had become a slippery coating on the black pavement. No matter how hard he pressed on the brakes, his car continued to slide into the intersection. He looked right and then left. That is when he noticed tons of steel in the form of a garbage truck heading for the driver's side door. The last thing his memory could produce was a vision of his love's smiling face. The sound of metal against metal soon followed, and the long-stemmed white roses went sailing through the air before everything went black.

Chapter One

"Rachel! Wake up! You're going to be late for your first day at your new school!"

I could faintly hear the sound of my Mother's voice as I slowly opened my eyes. Summer was officially over. My bare feet hit the carpet and I stumbled into the bathroom to transform myself into a presentable human being. Today was the first day of my senior year of high school in a completely new town. My family and I moved to Greensburg, Indiana, when my Father had to relocate for his job. We finally got settled a week before school started so my brother Daniel and I didn't have a chance to make new friends; as if starting a new school wasn't terrifying enough. I decided on a fitted gray t-shirt and the most comfortable pair of jeans I owned. I didn't want to show up looking like I was trying too hard. My makeup was kept to a minimum, a little blush and some mascara. My long, blonde hair was pulled back into a loose ponytail and I added some large, silver hoop earrings. I studied my look in the mirror, not too bad. I grabbed my backpack and headed downstairs.

"Good morning, Mom. Daniel, you ready to go?" My brother is two years younger than me and was starting his sophomore year. He pulled his attention away from SportsCenter on ESPN long enough to reply a tired, "Yes."

"You guys have a great first day! Call me if you won't be coming home right away."

"Thanks, Mom," I said. "See you later."

I pulled the car out of the garage and we met Dad at the end of the driveway.

"First day already, huh? Good luck and try to make new friends."

Daniel leaned over to the driver's side window. "We could say the same thing to you."

Dad chuckled and gave us a small wave.

Greensburg, Indiana seemed like a nice, quaint little town but it was nothing like the home we'd left in Charleston, South Carolina. When our parents informed us we would be moving, we were less than pleased. We would be leaving the life we knew; the town where we were raised, the schools we went to and the friends we'd made over the years. For Daniel's sake, I tried to make the best of the situation because he took the news the hardest. He's very shy and always had a hard time meeting new people. He had a good group of friends back home and didn't want to leave them behind. I tried to reassure him that we would keep our old friends and also make some new ones. It would be different not seeing those people every day, but I wasn't planning on cutting all ties with my old life. This especially applied to my best friend since grade school, Emily. We met on the school bus on the first day of kindergarten. Leaving Emily was hard, but we talk on the phone almost every day and I know our friendship is one that will stand the test of time.

Driving down the tree-lined streets into town, reality settled in; so did a small amount of nervousness. A new chapter in our lives was about to begin; a chapter I had not planned on. As we made our way toward school, we passed groups of friends who were hugging and greeting each other, preparing one another for the start of another school year. I followed the signs for the parking lot behind school and pulled my Ford Escape into a spot not too far from the entrance.

Daniel and I sat in silence for a few long seconds, trying not to be intimidated by our new surroundings.

BANG! The sound of something hitting the passenger door jolted us both. Annoyed, I leaned around Daniel to take a look and caught sight of a tall, dark-haired guy about my age, surveying the side of the car.

"Oh my god. I'm so sorry. I should've been paying closer attention." He crouched down and ran his fingers across the door. There was genuine regret in his voice. "Pretty good dent." He let out a heavy sigh. "Not the best way to start the school year."

I should've been thoroughly pissed since up until now there wasn't a single ding in the car. Oddly, the annoyance melted away. Not only was the guy great looking, but he also sounded genuinely upset. I must've taken too long to respond – but then who wouldn't be in shock from a tall, dark and handsome guy who just dented her door – because Daniel piped up. "It's okay, man. Nothing a body shop can't fix."

Daniel and I climbed out of the car and came around to inspect the damage. It wasn't so bad. A little putty, a little paint, and it would be good as new.

"Are you two new here?" He asked. "I don't think I've seen you around before."

"Yes, we moved here last week. I'm Daniel Conway. This is my sister, Rachel."

"I'm Evan." He thrust his hand out to Daniel and then to me.

"Uh, hi," I managed to squeak out. "Nice to meet you."

Evan smiled and for some reason my pulse took off on a hundred yard dash. "Nice to meet you, too. And again, I'm sorry about your door. Gives a whole new meaning to bumping into you." He raised his eyebrows.

"It's okay, really."

"Thanks for being so cool about it. Hope to see you around." He gave a small wave and blended into the crowd of students that gathered at the entrance.

"God, Rachel, could you please wipe the drool off your chin? I think you made it more than obvious that you were into him," Daniel teased. "Just don't forget, he screwed up your car."

Rachel shrugged. "Like you said, 'nothing a body shop can't fix'." Had she really been that obvious?

* * *

Daniel and I checked in at the office, and then headed in separate directions down the hall. Over my shoulder, I offered some sisterly advice, "Just be yourself. See you after school."

"Yeah, yeah. You too. Here's hoping you run into dream boat again." He held up his hand mimicking a toast.

I searched the numbers on the classroom doors until I found room 927. I took a deep breath and took a seat in the back of the room. Slowly, I scanned my surroundings. The popular girls were easy to spot. They wore the latest fashions and were texting on their cell phones while giving each other the low down on the amazing things they'd done over the summer break. I didn't mean to eavesdrop, it just happened. One of the girls was worked up about getting dumped by her boyfriend. Oh, young love. Next, I spotted the jocks sitting together talking about the football season that was already underway. The nerds also stuck out. They had congregated in the front of the room, close to the teacher, which came as no surprise. I wondered which group I would fit into. In Charleston, there were no specific cliques. If I had to put me and my friends in a category, I guess you could say we were the athletic type that also did well in our classes; sort of a blend of the groups I observed at this new school.

A few moments later, a petite brunette in a cute maxi dress sat down next to me. Judging by her appearance it was easy to tell which group she belonged to. She made small talk with a few of the girls but didn't fully engage in their conversations. Finally, she directed her attention to me.

"Hi. You must be new here. I'm Kate Moore." Instead of shaking hands, she offered a warm smile. "It's nice to meet you."

Somehow, I knew Kate and I would become good friends. "Is it that obvious? I'm Rachel Conway." I returned the smile. "It's nice to meet you too."

"It's a small town. New people stick out like a sore thumb." Kate laughed. "So Rachel, where are you from? I detect a small accent."

"Charleston, South Carolina. Dad got a new job here. We moved to Greensburg a week ago."

Kate's eyes lit up. "Wow. That didn't you give you much time to get to know the area. If you need anything or want a tour of the town, let me know. I'd be happy to help. I could show you around."

"Thanks so much, Kate."

When the bell rang, a familiar face scurried into the classroom. Evan. I couldn't take my eyes off of him as he made his way to the seat in front of me. My day just got a lot better!

"Evan, I thought you were right behind me," Kate said.

I sighed quietly with assumption. Kate and Evan was a couple. A surge of disappointment robbed me of the joy of seeing him. I was confused by the strong reaction; after all, I just met the guy twenty minutes ago. Had I been thinking clearly I would've realized that anyone that good looking wasn't available. *Pull yourself together, Rachel. Stop being so lame.*

"I had to stop at my locker. Made it just in time." He turned to Kate and his eyes widened when he discovered me sitting behind him.

"Rachel! Looks like we have the same homeroom."

I could have sworn he winked. Maybe I imagined it. "Good to see you again, Evan. I managed to find homeroom, my day is looking up." I playfully smiled, wondering if he picked up on the casual reference to the parking lot incident.

He grinned.

The morning announcements quieted the room. Pizza for lunch. Anyone interested in signing up for cheerleading needed to stop in the office. School pictures would be taken next week. The only thing I could focus on was the muscular back in front of me and the perfectly-styled head of dark hair that I wanted to run my fingers through. After attendance was taken, the real school day began.

I caught up with Kate in the hallway. "What do you have for first period?"

Kate looked over her schedule. "Geography."

"Me too."

"Good. Walk with me."

We made our way through the crowded corridor, and I nonchalantly brought up Evan. "So how long have you and Evan been dating?" That seemed like a safe question.

Kate wrinkled her nose. "Ew! He's my brother."

"Sorry," I laughed. Once the words escaped her mouth I was back on cloud nine.

Chapter Two

How one small body could hold this much excitement was beyond comprehension. I felt like I would burst if I didn't share my day. The minute I was home, I all but flew up the stairs into my bedroom. I dialed Emily before I slid out of my shoes, ditched my backpack on the floor, and fell across the bed.

Emily picked up on the first ring. "Rachel! How did your first day go?" There was happiness and exhilaration in her voice, it felt like a long-distance hug. "I thought about you all day."

"I miss you," I said straight away. It had been a great day. The only thing that would've made it better was if Emily was there.

"Miss you too, Rach. You can go into detail about how much your day sucked without me later. Right now I want the scoop. How was it?"

I laughed. "Surprisingly great! I met some really nice people and the teachers are pretty cool too." I paused. "The classes don't seem too hard."

"I'm sensing something more. Spill it!"

I grinned from ear to ear and joy erupted from my chest. "My car has a nice ding in the door. Funny story."

"What's so funny about a door ding?"

"It's more awesome than funny, really."

"Don't make me pull you through this phone, Rachel Conway. Dish the info, now!"

"The guy who dented my door, well…he has the bluest eyes I've ever seen. They remind me of the ocean near a tropical island."

Emily snorted a laugh.

"I'm serious, Em. You would not believe how incredible he is. He's tall, about 6'1" with a body made just for me." I wished. "His name is Evan. I wouldn't be surprised if he's the captain of the basketball team or something. He wore a blue-striped button-downed shirt with jeans that showed off his insanely cute butt. Short, dark hair. I love a man with dark hair and blue eyes. I'm sure I seemed like a psycho when we first met because I couldn't stop staring."

"He sounds hot! Did you talk to him much?"

"Not as much as I would have liked to. I did become friends with this girl in homeroom - Kate. As fate would have it, Evan is her brother. It couldn't have panned out better if I tried. I'm hoping we can all hang out together. And if he asks me out, I'll probably pass out."

Emily laughed because she knows I'm not exaggerating. I definitely would pass out. "Does Kate know you have the hots for her brother?"

"I didn't come out and say it, but any conscious person could probably tell."

"That's so exciting! Wish I was there to scope him out… and to catch you when you pass out."

They talked about Evan and how Emily's day had gone too, for over an hour.

I breezed through my homework, glanced at the clock and wished it was tomorrow.

* * *

My alarm startled me awake and I crawled out of bed refreshed, ready to start the day. What a change from my usual grogginess and sleep-walking through my morning. I decided to put more effort into my appearance. I considered the clothes the other girls wore yesterday and concluded that I needed to go shopping…soon. I rummaged through my closet, choosing a wine-colored pair of skinny jeans and an oversized white sweater. I slicked my hair back into a tight, high bun and put on some gold dangle earrings. Instead of just blush and mascara, I snazzed up my makeup routine with a bit of bronzer and some eyeliner. I slipped into some black flats and headed to the kitchen for breakfast.

"Whoa, Rachel! Look at you. Hot date after school?" Dad teased.

Before I could respond, Daniel did. "She probably is trying to impress Mr. Dream Boat. Right, Sis?"

I shot Daniel a look that said *Say anything more and you're walking to school.* "No, Dad, just trying to fit in."

Dad raised his eyebrows. "Mr. Dream Boat, huh?" He poured a glass of orange juice.

I filled my plate with scrambled eggs and slid into the chair across from him. "Daniel's just being a dramatic pest."

Daniel and I are very close with our parents. We always have been. They are involved with our lives and support us in every decision we make. Of course, they get on our nerves and embarrass us from time to time, but whose parents don't?

They would do anything for us and vice versa. Same applies to Daniel and me. We're only a couple years apart and have always looked out for each other. He has my back, I have his. Our little family has a bond that cannot be broken.

Before homeroom, I stopped at my locker. I ditched some of the books from my backpack and put the ones in that I'd need for my first few classes. I looked around at the other open lockers. Most had pictures of boyfriends or girlfriends or celebrity crushes, football schedules, calendars, you name it.

Evan peeked around my locker door. "Good morning, Rachel. I see we haven't scared you off yet. Decided to come back for more?"

He filled the small space between us; a hint of cologne came with him. Mmm. Nothing sexier than a man who smells good. "Yes, I came back for more." *Evan Moore.* She smiled even though her heart was skipping all over the place. "It takes a lot to scare me off. Actually, yesterday was a pretty good day. Everybody made me feel welcome. And your sister is so nice."

"Yeah, that's Kate for you. She's great. Anyway, I'm glad I ran into you this morning – not with my car door, thankfully." His mouth stretched into a playful grin at the memory of yesterday's fiasco. "Kate and I are having a party after the football game Friday night. We'd love if you could come. It would be a good way to introduce you to everyone." He leaned in close and the pulse that was skipping around, took off on a sprint. "Not to embarrass you or anything, but you have a little something in your teeth." He pointed to a spot on his perfectly aligned teeth.

Oh my god. Evan just invited me to a party. At his house. And I have something in my teeth. Note to self: Get a mirror for your locker. I tried to play it cool. "Yeah, I didn't have anything else going on after school on Friday and I love football, so of course, I'll be there. Plus, I heard the team is pretty good this year."

"Everyone has high hopes for the team this season. Last year they made it to the regional finals but lost by a last second field goal. This year we're out for revenge."

The way Evan lit up when he talked about football was so cute I could hardly stand it. Although, everything about Evan is cute. The sound of the bell cut into my joy.

"Time for homeroom. Can I carry your books?"

Seriously? Guys still did that? I was blown away and stumbled over my words. "Umm…no, that's okay. I appreciate the offer." I flashed him a smile and our eyes held for a few seconds. It felt like a thousand butterflies just took flight in my stomach.

Chapter Three

Friday night arrived and I could barely contain my excitement. Not only did I have the football game to look forward to, but more importantly, tonight was Kate and Evan's party. The air was chilly which called for a pair of jeans and a Greensburg Panthers hoodie. I figured that was the best option for cheering on the home team; not necessarily for impressing Evan.

Game time approached and I made my way to the stadium. Kate spotted me and waved me over to the concession stand. She quickly introduced me to her friends Holly and Nick, and Evan's friend, Will. I looked around for Evan but didn't want to seem too obvious.

Evan came around the corner with bags full of popcorn.

"Since it's the first game that we're going to together, I thought I'd treat." He handed a bag to everyone, except for me.

"Here you go, Rachel. By the way, you look great. That Panthers hoodie suits you." He smiled and finally handed me a bag of popcorn. My heart practically melted on the spot. It was just a hoodie and jeans, but he made me feel like a million bucks.

"Thanks, Evan." I lifted the popcorn bag. "And thanks for

the popcorn."

We found our seats; luckily I sat between Kate and Evan. The crowd roared when the home team took the field. Evan turned to me. "The other day you said you liked football. Have you gone to many games?"

"I used to go to all the games in Charleston. I've also been to a couple of NFL games. My Dad and I watch the games on Sundays. It's our bonding time."

His blue eyes sparkled. "A girl who loves sports. I knew you and I would get along. Let's just hope we can beat St. Mary's tonight. They're supposed to be tough."

At the end of the first half, Greensburg was head 10-7. It was so nice to see a majority of the town come out for the game and show their support for the Panthers. Apparently in Greensburg, football Friday night is a huge deal. That's what I love about small towns. Everyone goes all out wearing the school colors and cheer until their voices go hoarse.

After the final whistle blew, the Panthers won 24-21. I was quite impressed with the talent. Watching them play got me excited for the rest of the season.

When we got to our cars, Kate suggested I follow her and Evan to their house. "It's not far."

"Sure thing. Just don't let Evan drive like a maniac and lose me." I checked out Evan's flashy red sports car and was glad the little accident from the first day of school didn't damage it.

* * *

The two-story brick house was amazing with its perfectly landscaped lawn. Mrs. Moore had a lovely garden planted near the driveway and it was in full-bloom with red, orange, and yellow mums.

Evan met me at my car and opened the door. "Come on in, Rachel. I'll be glad to show you around."

I was in awe of the house…and Evan. The interior was just as beautiful as the exterior. High, vaulted ceilings covered the most impressive kitchen I've ever seen. Marble counter tops, stainless steel appliances, and wood floors welcomed me as I laid my coat on one of the kitchen chairs. Party food covered the counter so I assumed this wasn't their first post-game party.

I felt guilty that I came empty-handed. "Wish you would have told me to bring something. It didn't even cross my mind."

"Don't worry about it, Rachel. I enjoy hosting parties so I probably would have told you not to bring anything anyway."

Evan looked at me with those amazing blue eyes. "Would you like to see the rest of the house?"

With eyes like that, who would say no? "Lead the way."

He grinned.

First, we checked out the living room which was decorated with white furniture accented with colorful pillows and white walls were covered in expensive artwork. In the corner, a fireplace glowed while giving off a perfect amount of heat.

The staircase was lined with family portraits that ranged from Evan's great-grandparents to many of his cousins. As we proceeded up the stairs one photograph caught my eye. It was Evan and Kate sitting on a dock near a lake. There was a third person in the picture – a boy who looked a few years younger. He had a striking resemblance to Kate and Evan, and he had Evan's piercing blue eyes. "Nice picture, Evan. Who's this other guy?"

"That's Michael, our younger brother."

Evan's mood changed, but I didn't notice right away. "I didn't know you had a brother." I nudged him. "Why haven't you mentioned him?"

Evan shoved his hands in his pockets. "Michael died two years ago from a brain hemorrhage. He started getting severe headaches and couldn't stop vomiting."

I wanted to put my arm around him. I didn't know if I should or not, so I just listened.

"He was admitted to the hospital and died five days later." His voice cracked. "They ran all kinds of tests and determined his organs were good for donating. His heart went to a kid my age that needed it. It was what Michael would have wanted anyway. He was always thinking about how he could help others. He was my best friend. We did everything together. He was so full of life and had so many friends. He was active in all the school sports and was an excellent student. I always told him he could get into any college he wanted. Before he died, he told us he wanted to go to med school to become a pediatrician. Harvard or Yale would have been lucky to have him. He would have done great things. Sometimes I get really angry that he was taken so soon. He wasn't given the chance to show the world what he could do or what he was made of. Even though he was my younger brother, I looked up to him in so many ways. Ever since his death, I live my life how Michael would have lived his. He was the most caring, generous and humble person I have ever known."

Tears cracked the plane of his bottom eyelids and I watched as one ran down his cheek. My heart broke for Evan and I put a hand on his shoulder. "I'm so sorry, Evan. The way you talk about him shows that you truly cared for him."

"I did, Rachel. And I've never really talked about him that way to anyone since he died."

I'd been struggling with the idea of putting my arms around him, but the pure heartache I heard in his voice and saw in his face made me pull him close. For a few minutes, we stood in silence, chest against chest, our hearts beating against one another. In those moments, Evan felt like a friend, lover, and confidante.

Evan gently moved from my arms, but not before whispering, "Thank you."

* * *

Things were lighter, but different when we rejoined the party that was now in full swing. I recognized a lot of faces from the game. They greeted me like they'd known me forever. Evan mingled, going from room to room, being the perfect host, but his eyes never left me for long. Something special happened on those stairs, although I wasn't certain what it was.

Kate ran a plate of chips and dip in front of my nose. "You have to try this. It's so good!"

"What is it?"

"Just try it."

I dipped a chip into the bowl and took a small taste. "This is delicious." It was a version of spinach and artichoke dip that literally melted in my mouth. "Did you make it?"

"Yep. It's Mom's recipe." Kate surprised me with what she said next, I almost choked on the chip. "I see Evan told you about Michael."

I studied Kate. "He did. How did you know?"

"I could tell by the way Evan has been looking at you. I don't look at my friends the way he looks at you and I knew right away that he opened up. Call me crazy but I think my brother has a thing for you." She nudged my shoulder and I broke into a full grin. "Actually, I know he does. He told me," she said.

I felt something special between Evan and I, but I didn't want to assume anything. Now that Kate confirmed it, it put me in a mild state of shock. I wasn't sure what to do with the information or how to react. My heart raced and I couldn't stand still. She must've sensed my surprise and elation.

"Breathe, Rachel," she teased gently and wandered into the living room.

Evan filled the space vacated by Kate. I smiled and filled my lungs with his sexy scent. And for the first time, I acknowledged what I've known for awhile – I'm seriously attracted to this guy. He's not only gorgeous on the outside, but his inside is pretty spectacular too. The way he talked about his brother confirmed my thoughts about his character.

"I hope Kate wasn't saying anything bad about me just now." His cocky smile said he knew Kate would never sell him out. "What were you two talking about, anyway?"

The question prompted a blush to start in my chest, creep up my neck and into my cheeks. "We talked about the dip." It wasn't a fib. But my embarrassed-reaction surely said I'd left out a lot.

Evan pinned me with a look of *oh really?* The look softened and so did his voice. "What she said is true, you know? And I wanted to ask if you'd like to go out to dinner tomorrow night."

My knees buckled at the sound of his words and I struggled to stand up straight. The blue of his eyes deepened and I'm sure mine did too. He probably already knows my answer, but just to may sure I replied with, "I thought you'd never ask."

Chapter Four

Kate and I made plans to go shopping in the morning. Now that I had a date, it was as good of an excuse as any to buy some new clothes. The local mall in Greensburg is located about fifteen minutes from my house, so Kate swung by to pick me up. "Good morning, how did the rest of the night go?" I asked.

"It was good. Everyone pretty much filtered out shortly after you left." Kate kept grinning at me. "Come on," she said, "we have to find you a nice outfit for tonight. Once we cross that off the list, we can shop till we drop."

"You have great fashion sense, so I can't go wrong with you helping me pick something out." Kate really does have an eye for fashion. She has flawless taste in clothes and makeup. At the moment, she was wearing a burgundy top, tweed fall shorts with tights and wedge heels. I, on the other hand, decided to keep it simple with skinny jeans, boots and a black sweater.

Three hours and an insane amount of money later, we left the mall, bags in hand. I would definitely say our shopping trip was a success. With Kate's help I bought enough clothes for ten dates, but still had no idea which outfit to wear tonight. I smiled and knew what I had to do.

As soon as Kate dropped me off, I dialed Emily.

We got the small talk out the way – how much we missed each other, how senior year was even better than we expected, and how we couldn't wait to see each other again.

"Has Evan built up the courage to ask you out?"

Sometimes I feel like Emily knows what's going on in my life before I tell her. I guess it's that special connection known only to best friends. "Actually, he asked me to go out to dinner tonight."

There was genuine delight in Emily's voice. She was happy for me. "This is so exciting, Rach! Wish I was there to help you get ready. Where are you going and what are you going to wear?"

Come to think of it, Evan didn't say where we were going. Not that it mattered. I was just tickled to spend some time with him. "No idea where we're going and I'm not sure what to wear. I was hoping for your opinion." This wasn't just a garment-fixation. It was a chance to include Emily in my life, and looking good for Evan was a bonus. The great thing about social media is the ability to see things in real time. I showed Emily my purchases via Skype. It was as much fun as shopping with Kate. We laughed and carried on like we were in the same room.

* * *

Ten minutes till seven, I was ready and waiting for Evan. Luckily, my parents and Daniel went out to dinner across town so I didn't have to worry about them bombarding me with questions before he arrived. It had taken three hours to get ready. I spent extra time in the shower, shaved my legs until they were silky smooth, curled my hair to perfection and did my nails. With Emily's expertise I was dressed in a basic, belted black dress with long, sheer sleeves and a bold choice of hunter green tights. My black, suede ankle boots and a large, chunky gold necklace were the finishing touches. I was careful with my makeup, not too drastic. Hopefully, Evan would approve.

When he arrived right on time, he more than approved. His blue eyes rounded with surprise, at the same time his mouth dropped open. "You look beautiful, Rachel."

The tender way he said my name made all the fussing worth it.

He handed me a bouquet of white roses. It was the sweetest thing and it touched my heart. Evan had no idea he scored big points. "Thank you so much. They're beautiful. White roses are my favorite." I inhaled their amazing fragrance and put them in a crystal vase and sat them in the center of the dining room table.

It was all so magical! And the night was just getting started.

Evan took my hand and helped me into his Mustang. On his way to the driver's side, I noticed he was dressed in a pair of dark-wash jeans, a white and gray striped button down, and a black sport coat. Damn, he looked good.

"So, Evan, have you decided where we're going for dinner?" I asked while he fastened his seatbelt.

"It's a surprise." He winked. This time I didn't imagine it.

In a small way I was glad he kept the location a secret. I wanted to see what kind of place he picked without any input from me. Frankly, we could eat at McDonald's. It would still be a wonderful time and the company would be fantastic.

I'm surprised at how comfortable I am with Evan considering this is our first official date. I've never felt this at ease with a guy before. As if to reassure my thought, Evan reached for my hand and caressed my knuckles. At that moment, it felt like a thousand watts of electricity coursed through my veins.

"Rachel, I'm so happy to be spending tonight with you. I hope you like where we're going."

"Evan, you have nothing to worry about. There isn't anywhere else I'd rather be."

* * *

The closer we got to the secret destination, Evan told me to close my eyes. Without a seconds hesitation my eyes snapped shut. A few minutes later I felt the car come to a stop.

"We're here, Rachel. You can open your eyes."

I slowly let my eyelids open and I gasped when I discovered we were in the middle of Oakhill Park; a park outside of town. I spied a picnic table decorated with a white silk table cloth and at least a dozen candles. The trees surrounding the table were filled with white Christmas lights. Hanging from the trees was an assortment of Chinese lanterns varying in colors from pink, yellow, blue and purple. I don't think I've ever seen anything so romantic in my life. It looked like something you would see in a movie; except this was better, this was real life.

Evan's face beamed, he knows he's impressed me. Without trying to hide my excitement, I said what was in my heart. "Oh Evan, this is so beautiful. You took the time to do all this? This is by far the sweetest thing anyone has ever done for me.

Thank you so much."

"It's my pleasure. I wanted to do something special for you. And I can't take all the credit. Will helped me set this up."

"Be sure to thank him for me." I still couldn't believe my eyes. "I will remember this night for a very long time."

We sat at the picnic table and Evan reached under his bench and produced a wicker picnic basket filled with cheese and crackers, fruit, and a scrumptious chocolate cake. He also pulled out two wine glasses and a thermos of lemonade. Absolutely perfect!

As we dined, we talked about everything from our families to what we wanted to do with our lives. I talked about my former life in Charleston, the friends I'd left behind – especially Emily, and what Daniel and I were like as kids. I told him that after I graduate I'd like to go to college to become an optometrist. I've always been fascinated by the sense of sight ever since my grandfather went blind from glaucoma that went untreated. I shared my aspirations, my fears, and opened up to him like a rose in full bloom.

I learned a lot about Evan too. He talked more about Michael, and how the loss drew him closer to Kate. He explained that he didn't get to see his parents as often as he should. Both were doctors who worked late at the local hospital, and kept crazy office hours. He and Kate learned to take care of themselves at a very young age. His plan after graduation was to become a sports journalist. He'd always been a huge sports fan and writing for *ESPN The Magazine* or *Sports Illustrated* would be his dream job. Surprisingly, we talked about what size family we wanted down the road, which is unheard of on a first date, but it seemed like nothing was off limits. Coincidentally, we both wanted two kids, a boy and a girl. We talked until the sun set and we were surrounded by the glow of the Christmas lights. I glanced up and noticed how the sky was glittering with stars. "Oh wow! Look at the stars. I can see the Big Dipper."

Evan reached into the picnic basket and pulled out a large, red plaid blanket. He spread it on the grass. "Come here."

We laid on the blanket in silence and admired the beauty of the night. While I lay there, I noticed the gentle breeze swaying the leaves on the trees that had started to turn colors. The Chinese lanterns moved along with the wind. It felt like a dream, and Evan and I were the only two people left on the planet.

After a perfect evening of picnicking and star gazing, we left the park and found ourselves perched at my front door.

"I hope you had a good time tonight, Rachel. I know I did. Maybe we can do this again, soon?"

"I had a wonderful time tonight too, Evan. It couldn't have been better. And I'd love to go out with you again." I played with my house keys to buy some time.

At the click of the key unlocking the door, Evan leaned down and kissed me on the lips. My heart felt like it was about to burst from my chest. I've always wondered if that tingly feeling you get when you kiss someone truly special actually exists, now I know it does. Our kiss was the perfect ending to a perfect night.

I have concluded one thing as I walk into the house and up the stairs. I am in love.

Chapter Five

By the time Christmas came along, Evan and I had gotten pretty serious. The holiday season seemed to amplify our love for each other. One of my favorite things to do was to stroll along the streets of town, hand in hand with Evan, admiring all the holiday displays in the windows. There is something very romantic about Christmas lights. I've always felt that way, but now they remind me of our first date.

Tonight, Evan and I are going to downtown Greensburg for the annual Christmas tree lighting ceremony. Each year, one of the local tree farmer'ss donate the farm's largest tree to be decorated with thousands of lights to be displayed in the town square. I've been told it's a pretty big deal for everyone in the community. Perhaps not as impressive as New York City, but just as special. A lot of the local shops have sales, many restaurants offer free food, and they hold open-skating at Oakhill Park as long as the pond is frozen.

* * *

When we arrived downtown, the first stop we made was to buy hot chocolate. In my opinion, no Christmas activity is complete without a nice cup of hot chocolate. While we waited in line, Evan's friend, Will and his new girlfriend, Sara caught up with us.

"Hey you two lovebirds. We thought we might see you here." Will and Sara got in line behind us.

After we got our drinks, the four of us made our way to the crowded square. We spotted a lot of our classmates, some younger students, teachers and my parents.

The mayor of Greensburg always has a special member of the community stand on stage with him to start the countdown to the lighting. This year it is the school's superintendent, Mr. Thompson.

Mr. Thompson tapped the microphone. "Good evening, ladies and gentlemen. This year it is my pleasure to help with the Christmas tree lighting ceremony." He gestured around the crowd. "This has to be one of the best turnouts we've ever had, and for that we have all of you to thank." The crowd applauded and Mr. Thompson continued. "All right, everyone, let's begin the countdown. Five, four, three, two, one!"

By the time he got to one, the night was illuminated by thousands of Christmas lights. As if on cue, snow started to lightly fall from the sky. It was a spectacular vision. Now I understand why this is such a big deal in Greensburg. As we stared at the magnificent sight before us, Evan turned and took my hand.

"I love you, Rachel. I've felt this way for a long time now, but I wanted the perfect opportunity to tell you how I really feel."

My heart skipped a beat as I listened. Smiling, I blinked up at him. "I love you too, Evan." Our lips met and the rest of the world stood still while the Christmas tree provided a romantic backdrop.

* * *

Christmas Eve arrived. My family and I celebrate with a big meal. We open some presents and end the night by going to midnight mass. This year, Evan will be joining us. Evan fits in so well with our family and they love him as much as I do. Even Daniel has gotten pretty close with him. Every year, Mom makes herb roasted pork loin, red skin potatoes, spinach salad and pumpkin pie. Nothing different this year.

Evan arrived in the early evening and we began our meal. Everyone raved about Mom's cooking which always seems to boost her confidence. Evan said her pork loin is the most delicious thing he's ever tasted. When dinner was done, Evan offered to do the dishes, which earned him major bonus points with my parents. To be nice – and to open presents sooner – Daniel joined him at the sink.

Time to open gifts.

Everyone took a turn giving and receiving, and then it was time to open my gift from Evan. He walked to the tree, retrieved a small box from underneath, and handed it to me with a grin. The box was intricately wrapped with gold and silver paper. All eyes were on me. I slowly tore the paper away to reveal a small, felt jewelry box. Inside, was a gorgeous gold locket with a small white rose charm on the side.

"Evan, this is stunning! I love it." I stood up and thanked him with a kiss, before he secured the necklace around my neck.

"When I saw it, it screamed your name. I knew it had to be yours. I know how much you love white roses and the locket was just your style. I left the inside of the locket empty so you can add whatever pictures you would like."

"My turn," I said excitedly. "Sit right here. I'll be right back." I hurried to the bedroom, grabbed an envelope and returned to the family room. I handed Evan his gift and received a puzzled look.

Evans eyes widened with shock and amazement when he opened the envelope. Inside was a round trip plane ticket to New York City. He'd been talking about wanting to visit Columbia University because he'd heard it had a great journalism school. The only way he would know for sure was to make a visit.

"Rachel, this is too much."

"Evan, I wanted to buy the ticket for you. Columbia is your dream school."

Evan laid his forehead against mine. "You're the best, Rachel. Thank you. This means a lot to me." He pecked my forehead with kisses, then the tip of my nose before finding my mouth. With my parents and Daniel in the room, he brushed my lips with a brief kiss.

Knowing how much he appreciated my gift made me feel wonderful even though Columbia is about thirteen hours from Indiana. I can't imagine being away from Evan after high school, but I wouldn't ruin Christmas with those kinds of thoughts. When you love someone as much as I love Evan, it means you will do anything to make that person happy.

Chapter Six

Waiting for our college acceptance letters was one of the most nerve-wracking things I've ever gone through. Watching everyone get their good news only made me more anxious. Evan and I both applied to Columbia. He was very impressed with their school of journalism after his visit. He said the campus was beautiful and it was easy to get around. The professors he met with were helpful and knowledgeable in their fields of expertise. It wasn't until his second visit when he brought me along that I fell in love with Columbia too. The fact Evan would be there made me love it more. The SUNY State College of Optometry was equally impressive. I wanted nothing more than for Evan and me to receive our acceptance letters so we could celebrate along with our friends.

On Saturday morning, I was about to head out the door to take a jog when Dad came in with the mail.

"Rachel, honey, you might want to open this. It's from Columbia."

My heart started to race. I stared at the envelope realizing that whatever was written inside could possibly change my life forever.

"Well, are you going to open it?"

Mom joined us in the kitchen and raised her eyebrows.

They both watched and waited. Luckily the phone cut into the anticipation.

"Rachel, it's me." The second I heard Evan's voice I felt more at ease. "Did you get anything from Columbia today? I just got my letter but haven't opened it yet."

"I got mine too. I've delayed opening mine. Why don't you come over and we'll open them together?"

"I'll be right there." Fifteen minutes later he was at the door.

Letters in hand, we faced each other. Evan looked at me with those gorgeous blue eyes. With just a look, he calmed me and gave me a *you've got this* kind of expression. I smiled.

"One…two…three." We furiously tore at the envelopes and started reading.

Dear Ms. Conway,

So far so good.

Thank you for having expressed an interest in the Columbia College of Optometry.

You're welcome.

The Admissions Committee has given careful consideration to your application.

And…

We regret to inform you that we are unable to offer you a place in our first year class.

Oh my god. I didn't get in. Instant tears streamed down my face and it felt like I'd been punched in the stomach. I looked at Evan with blurry vision.

"Oh, no, Rachel!"

Evan dropped his letter and held me in his arms while I sobbed on his shoulder. The dreams I had of the two of us leaving Greensburg and starting a new chapter in our lives were shattered. All the hard work I put in this year seemed to be for nothing. I was heartbroken. I continued to sob uncontrollably, and Evan never let go. When I finally could speak, I asked, "What does your letter say?"

"I got in. But that means nothing to me now. I can go wherever you go. We'll go to the same school."

"Oh Evan, don't be ridiculous. You have to go to Columbia. I won't let you turn down your dream school. You've worked too hard not to go. Don't worry about me. I'll find another school and everything will be fine." I almost believed those last four words. "I'm so proud of you, Evan. You deserve this more than anyone I know."

"I love you, Rachel. Thank you for supporting me. It means the world to me. And I promise I won't let the distance come between us."

I hoped he was right.

* * *

The summer passed by in record speed. I got accepted to one of the local universities' optometry schools and classes will soon begin. I've been dreading the day when Evan leaves for New York. Tomorrow is that day.

Evan told me he wanted to spend some time with me before he left. So tonight we're going to dinner. I've been trying to keep a brave face and enjoy the evening but the pit of my stomach churns with the possibility that everything is going to change.

We finished a great meal at Schmidt's, our favorite restaurant in town, and headed back to Evan's.

The second I caught sight of all the boxes packed up and

ready for the U-Haul everything sank in. Tears started to come but I blinked them away. Evan has been unusually quiet. He's possibly feeling the same.

"So what are you thinking about? You've been really quiet tonight."

"Just thinking about starting classes and hoping I'll fit in okay in New York. A lot on my mind, I guess."

I placed my hand on Evan's. "Babe, you'll do great. Everyone will love you and you'll pass your classes with flying colors. I believe in you."

It seemed like everything I said went in one ear and out the other. Something was seriously bothering him. I decided to pry a little harder.

"Evan, what is it? What's wrong?"

Evan took a deep breath. When our gazes connected, he's not smiling and I'm suddenly nervous.

"Rachel, I know we said we would try to stick this out being in different states, but I've been thinking, and I'm not sure it's the best idea for us right now."

My heart sank. "What are you saying? Are you breaking up with me?"

"I just think we should take a break. It will be really hard for us to see each other with you in Indiana and me in New York. Plus, I think it will be easier for us to concentrate on school if we aren't together."

I couldn't believe my ears. My mind couldn't process what he'd said. I dropped my eyes to the floor and hoped it wasn't real.

"Rachel, please say something."

Evan cut into the fog of my misery. This was for real. We were breaking up.

I couldn't stop my voice from quivering. "I don't know what you want me to say right now. I love you so much and you just broke my heart into a thousand little pieces." Tears burned the back of my eyes, but I held them off. I was afraid once the first one fell they'd flood the place. "I thought we were going to stick this out. We planned that I would come to visit and for you to come home to see me. How can you just give up on us like that?" I was so angry and heartbroken. Amazingly the tears stayed put.

Evan stayed silent as though he was choosing his words carefully. "I just want to be able to fully dedicate my time and energy to Columbia. You of all people know how important this is to me and I want to do well this first year. I need to focus. A lot is riding on my first year grades. I could get an internship at one of the magazines. I hope you can understand that."

A million thoughts raced through my mind and the only thing I was capable of saying was, "Goodbye, Evan."

Without looking back, I walked out the door and numbly drove home. The love of my life just ended things and I didn't even see it coming. I must've drove on auto-pilot because I don't remember how I got from Evan's house to mine.

Somehow I made it to my bedroom. I dropped face first onto the bed and into my pillow. All the tears I held back poured out like a rainstorm in the spring. I couldn't imagine how I could just let go of Evan like that. He's my soul mate. I firmly believe he's the one. As I lay in bed, I wrapped my arms around me. There was a gaping hole in my heart like a huge piece of it had gone missing.

Chapter Seven

Breaking up with Rachel was one of the hardest things I've ever done, especially since I love her so much. But I had to do what was best for both of us, for our futures. I know she needed to concentrate on her studies in optometry school and I wanted an internship with *ESPN The Magazine* more than anything. Our career paths would require the best of us. I figured if we were single it would make things easier. After seeing the crushed look on Rachel's face, every bone in my body hurt. Surprisingly, she didn't cry. I know it took all of her strength not to. And it took all of mine to stay strong and see this through because I know she could've easily convinced me that staying together would work out just fine. There were a lot of outside influences that formed my decision. My parents had been successful in their lives and wanted the same for me. They encouraged me to start school with nothing holding me back. They wanted me to focus solely on school with no outside distractions. At the time, I agreed with them.

* * *

My first two years of school couldn't have gone better. I managed to get straight A's and make the Dean's list. I enjoyed the classes and seemed to impress my professors. Many of the classes required me to attend various sporting events and write a short article about them. Some of the comments I heard about my writing included, "he brings a new perspective to the game" and "unlike anything we've read before". If that didn't boost my confidence, nothing would.

At the end of the first semester of my sophomore year, they announced who would get internships at *ESPN The magazine and Sports Illustrated.* I really didn't care which one I got as long as I got one.

During my first year, I'd made a few new friends. Matt and Drew were in a lot of my classes and hoped for the same internships. We went to the same games and wrote about the same things. Miraculously, each of us brought a new idea to the table and our articles were so different even though they were based on the same event. I was fairly confident all of us would receive internships that summer.

In my first Sports Journalism class, I noticed a cute brunette sitting a couple seats down from me. I quickly struck up a conversation and we became good friends. Alison grew up in New York so instantly I was intrigued. The fact she was interested in the same things didn't hurt either. Seeing a girl in my classes was a nice change of scenery considering the majority of my classmates were male. Alison was thin, tall, and had the biggest brown eyes I've ever seen. Her favorite sport was football and she dreamed of being a correspondent for ESPN. She told me she wanted to be the next Erin Andrews, minus all the drama. She was smart and I knew she could do pretty much whatever she wanted. Her good looks would definitely not hold her back either. I could easily see her on TV, broadcasting from the sidelines of Monday Night Football.

Soon it was time for the internship announcements. The process at Columbia was to post the name of students who earned a spot just outside the Journalism 101 classroom. Unfortunately, Journalism 101 was the last class we had at the end of the week, which meant we had to spend the entire day on Friday stressing about whether or not we got the internship.

When the list was finally posted, we scrambled to find our names. Matt found his right away. Drew and Alison found theirs too. I didn't see my name. "Congratulations guys, looks like you're in," I said. I couldn't believe I'd been passed over for one of the treasured spots.

Drew crinkled his brows. "You're on there, buddy." He pointed to the list.

My heart raced. This was it. My dreams were coming true. At that very moment, the one person I wanted to share the news with was…Rachel. She would be so proud. She believed in me, challenged me to be the best writer I could be.

"Congratulations to you too, Evan," Alison said with a huge smile. "Looks like all our hard work paid off. This calls for a celebration! How about we go to the Dead Poet for drinks?"

* * *

Drew brought four shots to the table. He handed them out and raised his in a toast. "Here's to us. Showing the world, and more importantly – us, that we are damn good journalists with incredible futures. ESPN has no idea what we have in store for them!"

We clinked our glasses together and downed the shots

like champions. I was never a big drinker, but I had to admit, those shots were delicious. "Drew, what are these?"

He laughed. "They're called Sex with Alligators."

One shot led to another and another. Soon after, everything became a blur.

How I got from Dead Poet's to my bed isn't clear. My pounding head wouldn't provide the details. I sat up and tried to piece things together. Nope. Nothing. I rubbed my eyes and stumbled toward the bathroom. A snore, and not the deep manly kind, stopped me dead in my tracks. Sprawled out on the other side of my queen-size bed was Alison.

Chapter Eight

Oh shit. What happened last night? Trying not to wake Alison I quietly shut the bathroom door and turned on the shower. Instead of warm water, I shocked myself awake with a steady blast of cold. I closed my eyes and wondered what exactly happened last night. It appeared things had gotten out of hand. The last thing I could remember was doing shots with Drew, Matt and Alison.

After finishing my shower, I cautiously opened the bathroom door and tiptoed into the bedroom. To my surprise, Alison was gone.

I made a mental note to call Drew and Matt later; hopefully they could fill me in on the nights' shenanigans.

As if the headache wasn't enough, I had another reason to stay in bed all day – it was the anniversary of Michael's death. It was hard to believe it had been three years already. It seemed like yesterday that Kate, Michael and I were sharing our after-high school plans with each other and with our parents. I have no doubt that Michael would be proud of me for doing so well at Columbia. If he was still alive, I'm sure he would be making a huge difference at either Harvard or Yale.

The phone on the nightstand cut into my thoughts. Caller-Id said it was Kate.

"Hey, Kate, how are you?" I expelled a long breath. "I was just thinking about Michael."

"Good morning, Evan. I'm doing okay, I guess. I was thinking about Michael too. I miss him so much. And I had to call you to make sure you're doing all right." It was easy to tell she was on the verge of tears.

"I'm doing okay, but a little hung over. Have you talked to Mom and Dad today?"

"I have. And that's one of the reasons I'm calling. They found the name of the person who received Michael's heart. His name is Anthony. Anthony Drake."

Something incredible happened in that moment – hearing the name of Michael's heart recipient gave me a sense of closure. I've always wondered who carried a part of Michael with them; now I had a name. It didn't make losing Michael any easier but it was an assurance that he will live on.

Kate didn't have many details about Anthony, but she did know that he was twenty years old and suffered from cardiomyopathy. His heart wouldn't pump enough blood through his body and he wouldn't have survived without a new heart. Knowing my brother saved another person's life was a great feeling.

For another fifteen minutes, I reveled in the comfort of my sister's voice.

When I broke things off with Rachel, Kate was the one person who couldn't understand where I was coming from. She always told me that Rachel and I was a great couple and I would be an idiot if I ever let her go. Kate didn't speak to me for a good month after we broke up. Over time, she got used to the idea but she didn't mention Rachel's name in my presence – not to spare my feelings, but her own.

* * *

After my pounding headache lessened to just a dull ache, I decided to walk to the corner café to grab a cup of coffee. As soon as I opened my apartment door, Alison was there.

"Oh, hey, Evan. I was just about to knock. How are you this morning?"

"Hi, Alison." I rubbed my forehead. "I'll be okay once this headache goes away. Umm, did you want to come in?" I had no idea why she was there and it made me a little uneasy.

Alison paused for a moment. "Yeah, if that's fine with you. I just wanted to talk for a minute."

"Sure. Come in."

We sat at the kitchen table.

"Evan, I wanted to come over to say thanks for letting me crash here last night. We were all pretty drunk."

I was relieved that this wasn't going to be an awkward conversation. To make sure, I worked up the courage to ask the question that had been bothering me all morning. "Did anything happen between us last night?"

"Oh, Evan. No. You were all about Rachel last night. Everything we talked about or did reminded you of her. That's why I wanted to come over and talk. If I didn't know better, I would say you're still in love with her."

I sat in silence for a little bit, pondering the information. Alison was right. I never stopped caring for Rachel and she was always in my thoughts. I've wanted to call her to see how she's doing but never actually dialed her number. I guess I'm afraid she'll still be angry with me and won't want to talk. Not to mention Daniel would probably have some choice words for me if he knew I called his sister.

"I do still love Rachel, but I hurt her. The look on her face when I ended things made me want to take back everything I'd said and hold her in my arms. I thought I was doing the right thing for both of us. I wanted to focus on my first year here without any distractions. I wanted that internship. And optometry school is no cake-walk either. Rachel needed to give it her all and our relationship would've interfered." I winced. "I'm sorry. You didn't come here to listen to me go on and on about this."

Alison lifted an eyebrow. "Actually, I came here to talk you into calling her." She handed me the phone.

I was torn with indecision. Alison nudged me with her forearm. "Don't be scared. Just call her."

"I don't know."

Alison rolled her eyes. "Just do it all ready."

I didn't even have to think about the numbers, I punched them in like I dialed Rachel's number all the time. I glanced at Alison and she put her hand on my forearm. "You're doing the right thing," she said.

The phone rang twice. On the third ring, a strange voice answered.

"Uh, hi. Is Rachel there?"

"Rachel? Don't know anyone with that name. Looks like you've got the wrong number."

I repeated the numbers I dialed. "That's my phone number but there's no Rachel here."

I looked at Alison blankly. "She must've changed her number."

Alison's smile was warm. "I can tell how much you care about her, so don't give up."

"I won't."

Chapter Nine

Three years passed and I had no luck reaching Rachel. I convinced myself that she shut me out of her life and moved on. Who could blame her?

I focused all my energy on my career. It kept me busy and I turned out to be quite successful. The internship went great and I actually got hired on to work full-time at *ESPN The Magazine.* Many of my articles have been published and I got to interview a variety of famous athletes. The pay has been great too. I moved into a bigger apartment and have experienced all the wonderful things New York City has to offer.

Since my career consumed much of my life, I hadn't seen my parents or Kate in over a year. There were times when they wanted to come for a visit, but it just didn't work out with my schedule. I talk with them on the phone a few times a week, but I miss them more and more each time I hear their voices.

I don't think the job will let up anytime soon either. In fact, I have a meeting with the editor of the magazine today about some of my articles. He said he's been very impressed with me lately and wanted to discuss some additional responsibilities.

I decided to leave for work a little earlier this morning. With Christmas two weeks away, New York is lit up in grand fashion. Everything is beautiful and cheery, and I'm glad I had the time to take in the scenery. I made a point of walking past Rockefeller Center to see the big Christmas tree. There were some people already ice-skating.

As soon as I got to the office, I made a trip to the break room for a quick cup of coffee and then headed to the editor's office. Just as I expected, he spent a good deal of time raving about my work and how proud he is that I work for his magazine. I smiled with humility. I've worked damn hard to get there and now everything was falling into place. He informed me that they will be using one of my articles in every issue of the magazine. It will be called, Sports Talk with Evan, and my picture is to appear next to the headline. After the meeting I thanked him and walked back to my office grinning from ear to ear.

The red light on my phone was blinking indicating I had a missed call. Actually, it said that I had eight missed calls – five from my parents, three from Kate. Something was wrong. I called home and my dad answered on the first ring.

"Evan? I'm sorry, but we have some bad news. Your grandmother passed away this morning. The funeral is this weekend." He shared the details of what happened.

I loved my grandmother and the news of her passing brought me down from cloud nine to reality. My grandmother was ninety-seven and lived a long, wonderful life. Everyone back home knew her and loved her almost as much as her family did.

After I hung up, I headed back to my editor's office. He offered his sympathy and suggested that I take the remainder of the year off for the funeral and to catch up with family.

* * *

The drive to LaGuardia Airport was solemn despite Michael Buble softly singing his Christmas songs across the radio waves. I was happy to be going home but the circumstances were not ideal.

LaGuardia was packed. Couples walked hand-in-hand while their children either ran a few steps ahead or lagged a few behind. The smell of hot chocolate and peppermint coffee wafted through the air.

After making my way through security, I found gate A4. I had some time to kill so I pulled *The Times* from my carry-on and sat next to an older woman who was also involved in reading the paper.

"Hello," she said.

I smiled.

"You're heading to Indianapolis too?"

I nodded.

She was determined to engage me in conversation. "So what's taking you to Indiana?"

I peered over the newspaper. "My grandmother recently passed away. I'm going home for the funeral and to spend Christmas with my family." I'm generally not fond of making small talk with strangers, but the woman was sweet and I didn't want to hurt her feelings.

"I'm sorry," she said with sincere condolences. "I'm heading to my son's wedding. He gets married on New Year's Eve. They have a lot to do before then so I thought I'd come a little early to help out." She grinned so big it engulfed her face. "It's a mother's duty." She talked about her son and I could tell she was very proud.

"Congratulations. That's wonderful!"

The airline announced it was time to board.

"I'd better go, they called my section first," the woman said. "Have a wonderful holiday and I'm sorry to hear about your grandmother. By the way, I'm Joanie."

"Nice to meet you, Joanie. I'm Evan. Merry Christmas and enjoy the wedding." I shook her hand and watched her disappear with her carryon.

* * *

Home. It felt so good to walk through that front door. My parents heard me come in and squealed with delight. Tears welled in my Mom's eyes, and I'm pretty sure Dad had a few he sniffed back too.

I glanced around. Not much changed since I'd been away. Same Christmas decorations. The tree is in the same spot. And Mom is burning her sugar cookie candle like she always does this time of year. That same feeling of comfort eased the tension in my shoulders, just like it used to.

"Sweetheart, why didn't you tell us when your flight was coming in? One of us would have picked you up." Mom wrapped me in a hug.

"Getting a rental car is no big deal. Besides, it gave me a chance to take in the old neighborhood."

We sat in the living room to catch up. We exchanged stories about our jobs and I filled them in on what's been going on in my life in New York City. Kate was on Christmas break from her last year at Indiana University.

* * *

After changing into the black suit I'd brought along for

my grandmother's funeral, I started to make my way downstairs. When I passed the picture of Michael, Kate and me sitting on the dock, memories of our post-game party and how I opened up to Rachel came rushing back. I took a deep breath, closed my eyes, and relived that night.

When we arrived at the church I was surprised at how many people came to say goodbye to my grandmother. It was obvious that she had touched many people's lives in the community and they came to pay their respects.

We celebrated my grandmother's life in prayer and song. The cemetery was next. It was a tearful farewell that included everyone filing past the casket and placing a rose on top. Shades of reds, yellows and pinks were a spectacular send-off. One flower seemed to catch my eye more than the rest. There, on the cold, hard surface, sat a lone white rose.

My stomach dropped.

The crowd started to clear; that's when I spotted her. Rachel was there, looking more beautiful than ever.

The moment we made eye contact my heart clenched. She looked radiant. Her soft, blonde hair lay effortlessly on her shoulders and she wore a long, black coat and leather gloves.

I didn't think twice and hurried over without taking my eyes off of her.

"I'm so sorry for your loss, Evan," she said. "Your grandmother was a wonderful woman."

I could hardly form a coherent sentence. "Thanks for coming, Rachel. It really means a lot to my family and to me." I wanted to touch her, but was unsure how she'd react. "How are you doing?"

"I'm doing well. It's been such a long time since I've seen you. How are you doing?"

"It's been too long." I gave myself a mental scolding for allowing this much time and distance between us. "We have a lot of catching up to do. And you look magnificent, Rachel."

Rachel blushed and I was instantly reminded of this quality of hers that I fell in love with years before. "Would you like to grab lunch sometime while I'm home?" The words poured out before I had time to rehearse them in my head. I expected her to turn me down. To my relief, she said, "That sounds great. I'm pretty busy until New Year's Eve, but I can fit in a get-together sometime after Christmas."

"How is Thursday the twenty-seventh? We can meet at Schmidt's at noon if that works for you?"

She smiled. "Yes, that works for me. See you then."

Chapter Ten

The twenty-seventh couldn't come fast enough. When it finally did, I was a nervous wreck. I'd been pacing and clock-watching for the past couple of hours. It was finally eleven-forty five. Good thing, because I was wearing a path in the carpet.

I arrived at Schmidt's five minutes early and found Rachel already in a booth sipping a cup of coffee. She stood to greet me.

When I reached the table, I smiled and gave Rachel a quick hug. I slid into the booth and removed my jacket.

"It's good to see you again, Rachel. Did you have a good Christmas?"

"It was great. I got to spend a lot of time with my parents and Daniel. This year has been crazy busy, so it was nice to relax and enjoy the holiday." She shifted in her seat. "So how is New York? I hear you've been doing very well."

"It's been more than I could have ever imagined." I didn't want to talk about me. "How about you? What are you up to these days?"

She smiled. "I'm finishing up my last year of optometry school here in Indiana and have a job at a local optometrist's office. I've worked there for almost two years now. The people there are great and I'm doing really well in school."

"I'm happy to hear that, Rachel. I've always wanted the best for you." I meant every word. I wanted her to succeed and I was proud of her accomplishments. "What else is new?"

Rachel took a short breath and then placed her left hand on the table. It was hard to miss the enormous diamond on her finger. "I'm engaged and getting married on New Year's Eve."

It felt like my heart stopped beating and like someone punched me in the stomach. I was crushed. "This New Year's Eve? As in four days from now?" Regret squeezed my lungs so hard I could barely breathe.

"Yes. His name is Tony. We met when he came in for an eye appointment. He asked me out that day and we've been together ever since." She fished something from her purse and slid it across the table. "I'd really like you to come, but I'll understand if you don't."

I stared at the wedding invitation and was overwhelmed with the information. My thoughts went crazy and I still had hard time breathing. I cleared my throat. "I will definitely think about it."

Thank goodness the waitress arrived to take our order.

My heart was in distress, but I masked it with small talk and coffee. It was fifteen of the toughest minutes in my life.

Our food arrived and I went at my hamburger with a vengeance as a way to distract the ever-growing anguish in my soul.

Light reflected off of something gold – the locket I'd given Rachel for Christmas when we were still together. I zeroed in on the white rose charm still attached to the chain. How did I miss that she was wearing it? The answer wasn't too hard to figure out – I was too distracted by the extravagant diamond ring on her left hand. I took a sip of my coffee. "I didn't know you still had that necklace." I pointed to the locket.

"Of course I still have it, Evan. I love this necklace." She lifted the locket to look at it. "I wear it all the time."

The joy of seeing Rachel with the necklace relieved some of the grief that clutched my insides.

Our meal ended way too soon and the walk to her car felt like I was wearing cement shoes. I didn't want to see her leave. I didn't want our relationship to leave either. "Thanks for meeting me today, Rachel. It was so nice seeing you again." I wanted so say more – so much more.

Rachel leaned up to hug me and pecked my cheek with a kiss.

"Thanks for lunch." Her blue eyes sparkled with indiscernible emotion. "I'm glad we did this. And please think about coming to my wedding. It would be nice if you came."

A nod was all I was capable of because my voice would reveal the depth of my angst.

* * *

I sat in the driveway for what seemed like forever, going over every word of Rachel and my conversation. *She's getting married* blared in my brain with such velocity that my head felt like it would explode.

Too much coffee at the restaurant finally made me go inside.

Kate hollered from the couch. I signaled that I'd be there in a minute. In the bathroom, I leaned against the sink and stared at my reflection in the mirror. I'd been a fool. A giant fool. But it was too late now. Rachel had moved on.

I slid next to Kate and placed the invitation on the coffee table.

"Did you know about this?" I asked soulfully.

Kate eyed the invitation. When our eyes met, I knew the answer before she confirmed it. "Yes, I did. I thought there was a chance you would see Rachel while you were home and I wanted to let her tell you." A puddle of tears clouded her eyes. "I'm going to the wedding. Maybe you and I could go together."

I sat in silence while I let the initial shock wind down. Part of me wanted to take my heartache out on Kate for knowing and not telling me. But she wasn't to blame for any of this, I was. Besides, I wouldn't have believed it anyway. I had to hear it from Rachel.

"Kate, I'm not sure I can go to the wedding. I realize I made a mistake letting her go and it would be too hard to listen to her pledge to love someone else for all eternity."

"Evan, I know how hard this is, but I also know how much Rachel means to you and that you want her to be happy."

I did love Rachel. And I wanted her to be happy. Neither admission would keep me from falling apart.

Chapter Eleven

New Year's Eve arrived and I still hadn't made a decision whether to go to the wedding or head to the airport. My heart wasn't sure it could handle hearing Rachel repeat vows with someone else.

After a few grueling hours of uncertainty, I knew I had to go. I had to put my feelings aside and be happy for Rachel. Kate was right. I broke her heart and Rachel had the right to be happy again. No matter how much it hurt, I had to show my support for her new life.

Kate and I climbed into the rental car. As soon as I pulled out of the driveway it started to snow; lightly at first, but seemed to increase with every block we drove. I pictured Rachel smiling at the snow on her wedding day. She loved snow. As I drove down the winding roads, I couldn't help wondering how different things would be if I hadn't broken things off with her. Would she be marrying me today instead of Tony? So many questions raced through my mind, but few answers.

St. Andrews Church was decorated with Christmas lights, candles, and hundreds of roses. The decorations were so Rachel; classy, romantic, breathtaking. And the incredible scene made the air seize in my lungs. I wasn't sure how I would get through this.

Kate and I managed to work our way through the crowd and grab a program. Out of the corner of my eye I caught a glimpse of a familiar face. Standing at the entrance was Joanie, the woman from the airport. She was carefully pinning boutonnieres on the groomsman's lapels.

"There's the mother of the groom," Kate whispered.

"I know," I said so quietly I was pretty sure Kate hadn't heard. I made eye contact with Joanie and gave her a small wave. Her mouth dropped open, but then she smiled and gave me a return wave before resuming the task of pinning on flowers.

I glanced over my shoulder as we entered the church. Joanie? Really?

Kate and I slid into a pew toward the back. I tossed the program aside, but then curiosity made me pick it up and open it.

Mr. and Mrs. Ray Conway
and
Mr. and Mrs. Ian Drake
Invite you to share in the joy of the marriage
uniting their children
Rachel Marie Conway
and
Anthony Lewis Drake

Unable to read on, I closed the program. Again, I laid it aside. Something in my subconscious poked me hard. Anthony Lewis Drake. It felt like someone dumped a ton of bricks on me. Anthony Drake is the name of the man who received Michael's heart. I looked at Kate and realization hit her too. I was overcome with emotion and couldn't think. Rachel was marrying Anthony Drake! The look on Kate's face said she was struggling to connect the dots too.

"Kate, I don't know if I can stay. This is just too much. I'm sorry, but I have to go." I didn't wait for Kate's response. I had to get out of there before I did something stupid. I climbed into my car and drove out of the parking lot like a bat out of hell. Tears came hard and fast and I didn't try to blink them away.

Somehow I managed to make it home without wrecking the car.

I flew up the stairs, dragged my suitcase from the closet, and threw my stuff in. I slammed it closed and took off for the airport.

Millions of thoughts clouded my brain as I sped down the interstate, hardly noticing the deteriorating road conditions. Before I caught the exit that would take me to the airport, I was struck by a painful reflection – I was running away from Rachel all over again.

If I didn't go back and tell her how I felt I would never forgive myself and I'd be filled with regret for the rest of my life. If I hurried, I could make it back before she said "I do".

I pulled a U-turn and headed back to town. A neon sign at a flower shop caught my eye. I didn't want to waste precious minutes, but this was important…so, so important. I ran in, money in hand, and left in a hurry with a bouquet of white roses.

The snow tumbled from the sky in heavy, wet flakes making the roads an icy mess, but it was actually quite beautiful. The closer I got to the church, the harder my heart pounded. Just a couple more traffic lights and I would be able to tell Rachel how I felt and hopefully things would change. I ran through the words I would say to her over and over again, and then…everything went black!

Chapter Twelve

I couldn't believe it was my wedding day. As I stood in front of the mirror with my wedding gown, staring at my reflection, my heart was heavy. Seeing Evan again complicated everything. It made me question if what I was doing was right. Could I go through with the wedding? All the feelings I had for Evan in high school never really went away. I still loved him. But now there was Tony. I loved him too. He had been such a wonderful guy and treated me like a princess from the day we met. Why did I have these feelings of indecision today of all days? This was supposed to be the happiest day of my life and now all I felt was confusion.

"Rachel," Emily said, rapping lightly on the bathroom door, "It's almost time. Are you ready?"

A small gush of air came from somewhere close to my soul. I opened the door and tugged Emily inside. "Emily, I'm so confused." I buried my face in my hands. "I don't know if I'm doing the right thing."

Emily wrapped me in a hug. "Rachel," she said soothingly, "is it because you met with Evan the other day?"

"Yes. I just wish there would be a sign pointing me in the right direction. I need to know if this is what I'm meant to do."

My Dad knocked and then peeked around the door, panic etched his expression. "Dad, what is it?"

"Rachel, Evan has been in a serious accident. His car was hit by a garbage truck. It flipped over and he's at Decatur County Memorial Hospital."

I looked at Emily and knew that this was my sign. I couldn't risk losing my first love.

"Dad, I...Dad..." My heart pounded so hard it hurt. Tears blurred my vision. "Please tell Tony...Oh God! Please tell Tony that I have to go to Evan. And I hope someday he'll understand. I have to go to the hospital."

Frantic, I ran from the church, wedding dress dragging across the snow, tears running down my face, and repeating "I'm coming Evan."

I heard my Dad calling after me, but I didn't wait. I climbed into my car and took off as fast as the road conditions would allow. With every icy mile, the more scared I became. The thought of losing Evan was unbearable. I couldn't imagine life without him.

I arrived at the hospital, mascara smudged beneath both eyes, my nose red crying from crying, and my veil halfway off of my head.

The volunteer behind the emergency room desk took one look at me and her eyes widened.

"Evan Moore, please."

I know it pained the woman to ask, especially in my haphazard tearful condition, but she had to. "Are you family?"

"Yes, I'm his fiancée."

The woman looked at the veil slipping from my head and then at the dress that was now a soggy mess. She smiled with concern and directed me to Evan's room.

My heart clenched when I saw him lying in that hospital bed. His face was bruised and he had a row of stitches near his hairline.

I took his bandaged hand. "Evan, sweetheart, can you hear me?"

Evan slowly moved his head and opened his eyes. "Rachel..." he said in a raspy whisper, "...what about the wedding?"

I smiled tenderly. "I couldn't marry Tony. I'm still in love with you. In fact, I've never stopped loving you. And I will for as long as I live. You're the one I want to be with forever."

I bent down and gave Evan a soft kiss. He took my hand and put it on his cheek.

"Rachel, you've made me the happiest man on earth."

Epilogue

I knew just the place to propose. With Rachel beside me, I drove into Oakhill Park. I had spent the entire morning getting everything ready for the most important night of my life. I recreated the night we shared all those years ago. The decorations were the same: Christmas lights dangling from the trees, Chinese lanterns providing a colorful backdrop, and as many white roses as I could afford.

Rachel gasped and leaned over to give me a soft, passionate kiss. "Evan, you did all of this again? How romantic!"

I got down on one knee and took her hand. "Rachel, you mean more to me than life itself. And I can't imagine spending one day without you. I love you more than you will ever know."

She smiled at me, love sparkling in her eyes. "I love you too, Evan."

I fished a felt box from my coat pocket and held it out to her. I opened the box to present her with a small, white rose. "Will you make my dreams come true and be my wife?"

Rachel picked the rose from the box and tucked inside was a square-cut engagement ring. Her mouth dropped open and she smiled the biggest smile I've ever seen.

"Yes, Evan, yes! A thousand times yes!"

Looking back, that accident was one of the best things that ever happened to me. It brought me back to reality and to what my life had been missing those years without Rachel. Hearing her voice while I lay in that hospital bed cured my broken heart, and then some. The touch of her hand on mine took all the pain away and I felt nothing but relief. And it brought me love; a love greater than anything else I've ever experienced, a love that would stand the test of time and could never be broken.

About the Authors

A fifty-something wife and mother, **Nancy Ricker** lives a simple life in small town America. Following a fulfilling nursing career of 38 years, she continues to work and volunteer for pure enjoyment in less stressful environments. Newly found freedom prompted her to cross a few stubborn items off of her bucket list, and a challenge presented by a successful author and friend resulted in this literary work. Nancy's large, endearing family and diverse cluster of friends keep her journey adventurous and entertaining.

Jan Romes grew up in a small town in Ohio with eight siblings who remain a constant source of love and entertainment. Married to her high school sweetheart for more years than seems possible, she is also a proud mom, mother-in-law, and grandmother. Jan loves to read, write witty romance, take nightly walks with an incredible group of supportive friends, and grow pumpkins and sunflowers.

Laura Ricker, a twenty-seven year old first time writer, lives and works in Columbus, Ohio. She spends her free time amongst friends and family and often daydreams about where life will take her. Owning a winery, living on the beach, and traveling the world are on top of her to-do list. Currently living the single life, Laura is hoping to find her version of Mr. Dream Boat and live happily ever after. Until then, she will continue to enjoy whatever life throws her way.

Made in the USA
Middletown, DE
18 December 2016